PRAISE FOR

The Beginning of *her* Becoming

"*The Beginning of Her Becoming* is raw, real, and redemptive. With unflinching honesty and spiritual depth, Carla Calizaire gives voice to the battles so many women carry in silence — heartbreak, single motherhood, the ache of a life that didn't unfold as planned. And then she takes us somewhere even more powerful: into the surrender, the faith, and the becoming that waits on the other side. This is more than a novel. It is permission to heal."

— Rev. Dr. Elaine M. Flake, author of *God in Her Midst: Preaching Healing to Wounded Women;* Pastor Emeritus, The Greater Allen A.M.E. Cathedral of New York

"*In The Beginning of Her Becoming*, Carla Calizaire invites us into a sanctuary of the "sacred ordinary" where every tear and every detour is a sign pointing toward a deeper well. This is not merely a riff on the biblical woman at the well — it is a granular excavation of the heart's deepest thirsts. She captures the "shattering" of a life with a poet's precision and a pastor's grace, reminding us that we often meet the Living Water not in our triumphs, but in our rubble. If you've ever felt like your story was over, let Chelsea Stevens lead you back to the beginning. With God, our breaking is merely the opening through which the Spirit finally rushes in."

—Leonard Sweet, author of *Jesus Imagination;* professor, preacher, publisher, proprietor

The Beginning of *her* Becoming

The Beginning of *her* Becoming

A novel of faith, fire, and the fight to heal

Carla Calizaire

Scripture quotations marked (NLT) are taken from the Holy Bible, New Living Translation, copyright © 1996, 2004, 2015 by Tyndale House Foundation. Used by permission of Tyndale House Publishers, Carol Stream, Illinois 60188. All rights reserved.

Scripture quotations marked (NIV) are taken from the Holy Bible, New International Version®, NIV®. Copyright © 1973, 1978, 1984, 2011 by Biblica, Inc.™ Used by permission of Zondervan. All rights reserved worldwide. www.zondervan.com. The "NIV" and "New International Version" are trademarks registered in the United States Patent and Trademark Office by Biblica, Inc.™

LIBRARY OF CONGRESS CATALOGING-IN-PUBLICATION DATA:
Names: Calizaire, Carla, author.
Title: The Beginning of Her Becoming: A novel of faith, fire, and the fight to heal / Carla Calizaire.
Description: [New York]: Vine Publishing, 2026.
Identifiers: LCCN 2026906870 (print) | LCCN 2026906870 (ebook)
ISBN: 979-8-9891446-9-3 (trade paperback)
ISBN: 979-8-9952257-1-3 (ebook)
Subjects: LCSH: **Christian fiction**—Fiction. | LCGFT: **Romance fiction**.
Novels.

Published by Vine Publishing, Inc.
New York, NY
www.vinepublish.com
Book Design by Taneki Dacres
Printed in the United States of America

To my parents, whose sacrifices made so much possible—and to my sons, Jayson and Christian, who make it all worthwhile.

Note *to* Reader

I didn't write this novel to simply tell a story.

I wrote it to invite you—yes, *you*—to reflect, search, and perhaps even find yourself in the quiet, complex, and courageous journey of Chelsea Stevens.

Her story is fictional, but her battles are very real. Like many of us, Chelsea finds herself in a head-on collision with life— where broken dreams, unexpected turns, and quiet moments of surrender shape her into the woman she was always meant to become.

This is not just a novel. It's a mirror. A companion. A quiet nudge that says: *No matter how dark the moment or how desperate the detour, you still have the power to choose. To trust. To rise. To begin again.*

Through Chelsea's story, my prayer is that you will see more than one woman's struggle—I hope you see your own resilience, your own becoming, and your own divine potential. And I hope, most of all, that you'll come away knowing that with God, where you are now is never the end.

It's only the beginning.

May you find revelation, healing, peace, and renewed hope as you journey hand-in-hand with Chelsea.

When the Shattering Begins

It wasn't a moment Chelsea could explain—only one she would never forget.

The silence in the house was thick. Not peaceful. Not gentle. But heavy. Suffocating. Like something holy had left, and all that remained was a shell of what used to be.

The dishes were still in the sink. The laundry was half-folded. Her Bible lay open on the kitchen table next to the untouched cup of tea she had made hours ago. A verse she had once found comfort in now stared back at her like a dare:

"Weeping may endure for a night, but joy comes in the morning."

But what if the morning never comes?

Chelsea had asked that question more than once. In the quiet. In the chaos. In the moments between heartbreak and hope. She had stood in front of mirrors and people, pretending to be okay when her soul was unraveling.

But not today.

Today, something in her had finally cracked open—not with defeat, but with decision. She wasn't sure what tomorrow would look like. But she knew what *couldn't* continue: the shrinking, the apologizing, the pretending.

She was done waiting for someone else to rescue her. She was done rehearsing pain and calling it faith. And most of all, she was done asking for permission to live.

It was time to face the rubble. And maybe—just maybe—rebuild.

This is the moment her story begins.

Not with the fairy tale.

Not with the breakthrough.

But with the breaking.

Because sometimes the most sacred journeys don't start with miracles.

They start with surrender.

* * *

"Everyone, may I have your attention?" Maya called out, tapping her glass lightly with a fork. The clinking echoed just enough to quiet the room. A warm smile spread across her face as she raised her glass. "It's time for a toast."

She turned toward Chelsea with genuine affection. "To Chelsea and Collin—may every dream you've ever dared to dream come true. Chelsea, I hope you get that beautiful home filled with laughter, love, and maybe even a few little ones running around. I hope your career soars—you deserve that corner office with a skyline view. And while you're at it, throw in the white picket fence and a golden retriever. But most of all, may your marriage be filled with joy, resilience, and deep love—lasting well into your silver-haired years."

Before anyone could respond, Jessica chimed in with a

mischievous grin. "Okay, but are we just going to ignore the most important part? If you're signing up to spend the rest of your life with one man, he better be able to rock your world behind closed doors. Ladies, let's raise a glass to passion—and a great sex life!"

Laughter erupted across the room as Chelsea blushed, fanning her face. "I don't think that's going to be a problem," she replied playfully. "Have you seen Collin's arms? Let's just say they're good for more than just lifting moving boxes."

"Aww, no," Sarita groaned, covering her ears dramatically. "That's way too much information!"

Maya raised an eyebrow and leaned in with a smirk. "Not at all. That's exactly what we're here for. This is a bachelorette party, remember? We want the juicy details!"

"I second that," Danielle added, her eyes gleaming. "So . . . what exactly has he been lifting besides boxes?"

Chelsea grinned, her eyes sparkling with mischief. "Wouldn't you like to know?"

With theatrical flair, Maya reached beneath the table and revealed a bold red-and-black gift bag overflowing with ribbon and lace. "Chelsea, allow me to contribute to your honeymoon toolkit. I brought a few—let's call them enhancements—for you and Collin to enjoy after the 'I dos.'"

Sarita gasped, half-laughing, half-shocked. "Maya! I always knew you had a wild side."

Danielle sprang from her chair and plucked something from the bag. "Nothing wrong with keeping things spicy. I've been married for a year now, and my husband still rushes home to me like we just started dating. Gotta keep him on his toes— sometimes literally."

"Wait . . . are those actual handcuffs?" Chelsea asked, wide-eyed.

Danielle grinned and nodded. "Handcuffs and the matching outfit."

Sarita pointed an accusing finger while laughing. "Okay, so Maya's not the only undercover wild child in this group."

Danielle waved a hand dismissively. "Call me what you want, but our connection is still as strong as ever. If a little fun keeps that spark alive, I'm all in."

Chelsea's expression softened. "I don't know if Collin would go for the handcuffs, but I do hope that thirty years from now, he still rushes home to me like it's our wedding night."

"Amen to that," Maya said, raising her glass. "When I get married, I hope my husband still thinks I'm a total knockout at ninety-nine."

Sarita rolled her eyes with a laugh. "Ninety-nine and hot? Come on, Maya, let's stay in the realm of reality."

"It is reality," Maya shot back. "At least in my story."

Chelsea leaned over and peeked deeper into the gift bag, her curiosity getting the best of her. She pulled out a sleek leather whip and raised an eyebrow at Maya. "You don't have to worry, Maya. Sean only has eyes for you. Just get him down the aisle, and you're golden."

She held up the whip playfully and added, "And if he hesitates, you can always borrow Danielle's cuffs and gently persuade him."

The room erupted again in laughter, the air buzzing with friendship and flirtatious fun.

Sarita raised her voice above the chatter. "Okay, ladies, my margarita is melting and my buzz is fading fast. Can we please resume the real mission here?" She lifted her glass high.

"To Chelsea and Collin—may your love always be deep, your laughter loud, and your bond unbreakable."

The group echoed together, voices full of love and joy: "Cheers!"

* * *

That night, Chelsea laughed until her cheeks ached and her stomach hurt. But as the party quieted and the gifts were packed away, she couldn't ignore the subtle throb in her chest—the kind that whispered what no one else could hear.

There was a flicker in her eyes as she washed off her makeup. A tiny question she didn't want to answer. Not yet.

Everything was perfect. And yet . . .

Sometimes, the unraveling begins long before the thread ever breaks.

And sometimes, the loudest warning signs come in the quietest moments.

Chelsea didn't know it then, but that night marked the end of the dream—and the beginning of her becoming.

The Storm We Hid In

Three years later

"You can do this . . . You can do this," Chelsea whispered under her breath, each word an anchor against the storm rising inside her. She moved slowly, deliberately, her footsteps unsteady as though wading through quicksand. Her eyes locked onto Collin, who was sweeping the floor with an eerie calm, oblivious to the turmoil building behind her determined gaze.

For months, she had rehearsed this moment—carefully crafted lines playing over and over in her mind like a well-worn script. But now, standing just feet from him, her words abandoned her. They lodged in her throat like stones, choking her courage.

Collin looked up, unmoved. "What do you want?"

The question pierced her. With a blank stare, she blurted out the truth. "I want a divorce. I can't live like this anymore. I'm done."

Without even looking at her, he continued sweeping. "Then leave."

"I'm not going anywhere," she said, her voice cracking. "We can live in separate rooms until the details are sorted, but know this—I'm filing first thing in the morning."

That stopped him.

"No," he snapped, his voice rising like a sudden storm. "You're not staying here. You want out? Then get out. Take all your crap and leave!"

She stared at him in disbelief, the cruelty of his words cutting deeper than usual. She was pregnant with their second child.

"I'm not leaving," she repeated, her voice now trembling. "I worked just as hard as you did for this home. It's mine too."

Without waiting for another outburst, she turned and walked away, unsure of what her next step would be. She had spent hours preparing her speech but never once imagined what would come next.

Her heart pounding, she left the kitchen, her breath short and shallow, her legs shaking beneath her. She turned the corner, sprinted up the stairs, and locked herself in their bedroom. Her body pressed against the door as if that alone could keep Collin's fury out. She didn't know what to expect—his temper could be unpredictable, sometimes silent, sometimes explosive.

She glanced over at her sleeping two-year-old son. His peaceful face was untouched by the chaos that surrounded him.

He doesn't even know his life is about to change, she thought. He has no idea.

Crossing the room, she knelt beside him and gently stroked his cheek. "God . . . what have I done?" she whispered. "How am I going to raise two children on my own?"

Before she could collect her thoughts, the door crashed open with a deafening bang.

"Didn't you hear me?" Collin roared. "Get the hell out of my house!"

"Collin, stop!" she cried. "You're going to wake up Daniel!"

"I don't care! Get out!"

His eyes burned with rage. For the first time, Chelsea saw something in them she had never seen before—hatred. Contempt. A terrifying emptiness. He looked around the room, searching for something—anything—to hurl. His eyes landed on a vase of dried roses, a gift from months earlier after a previous attempt to leave.

He grabbed it.

"Why are you still standing there?" he bellowed. With one furious motion, he hurled the vase at her.

Chelsea instinctively turned, shielding her stomach. She was determined—he would not harm her unborn child.

The vase shattered at her feet.

Daniel woke up screaming. "Mommy!" he cried. His tiny eyes flickered between his parents, confused and frightened.

"Collin, please," she pleaded. "You're scaring him. Just leave."

But before she could finish, Collin lunged at her, knocking her to the ground.

"I'm not going to let you destroy my family," he hissed into her ear.

Tears welled in her eyes as a sharp pain spread across her abdomen. "My baby," she murmured through clenched teeth. "My baby . . ."

Collin's hand pressed against her belly, the other around her neck. "It's my baby too."

Daniel shrieked, "Mommy! Mommy!" and began hitting his father, trying to protect her.

As Collin turned his head toward his son, Chelsea seized the moment—she kicked him hard between the legs.

He stumbled back in agony.

Without hesitation, she grabbed Daniel, bolted down the stairs, and raced to the front door. Her handbag and keys were by the entrance, waiting like old friends. She snatched them up and reached for the knob, but Collin was there again, blocking her escape, trying to pull Daniel from her arms.

"Let go of him!" she shouted. "Let go!"

"No! You're not taking my son!"

"You said you wanted me gone. Well, I'm going! Now let go!"

Daniel was sobbing hysterically, his cries now screams of terror. He clung to Chelsea, pounding on his father's arms. "Daddy, stop! Let me go! I want Mommy!"

Something in Collin's eyes shifted. He froze. And in a moment of clarity—or guilt—he released his grip. "Chelsea," he begged, breathless and broken. "Please don't go. Don't leave. I'll go."

But she turned away. She knew better. If she stayed, he would come back. He always did.

What if next time he didn't stop?

"I'm leaving," she said, her voice hollow but firm.

And with nothing but the clothes on her back, a toddler in her arms, another child in her womb, and nowhere to go, Chelsea walked out into the night.

* * *

Chelsea drove aimlessly for a while, too shaken to make a plan.

Her parents lived nearby, but she couldn't face them—not yet. No one knew how bad things had become. How could she explain it? And in truth, she wasn't ready to explain anything to anyone. All she needed was a bed. A moment to breathe. A few hours to fall apart.

She pulled into the first hotel she saw, only to be met with disappointment. No vacancies. She had forgotten the Goodwill Games were in town.

Of course.

She drove to another, then a third. Same answer each time.

"No rooms available."

With every *no*, her strength slipped away.

By the fourth rejection, she stood at the front desk trembling, her voice barely above a whisper. "Please . . . I just need a place to sleep. Just for tonight."

The clerk looked at her apologetically. "I'm sorry, ma'am. I truly wish I could help, but we're fully booked."

Her heart sank. "Daniel," she whispered, "Mommy has to put you down."

But he clung tighter. His fear hadn't left him—just like hers hadn't.

Chelsea's body gave in. Her knees buckled. Her vision blurred. She slid down the wall of the hotel lobby and curled up on the floor.

"God," she whispered through sobs, "please . . . just help me get through this night."

The clerk called out, "Miss, are you alright? Do you need help?"

But Chelsea couldn't answer. The world was spinning. Her heart was pounding. Her thoughts unraveled.

"I'm pregnant . . . I'm supposed to be happy. I'm a good person. Isn't good supposed to come back to me?"

Daniel touched her face, his tiny hands wiping away her tears. "Mommy," he whispered. "I want to go home now."

A voice inside her—faint but firm—rose above the chaos: *Get up. You have to do this. For him. For the baby. No one can take from you what God placed inside you.*

She pulled herself together, clutched Daniel's hand, and walked out of the hotel with every ounce of willpower she had left.

Back on the freeway, she saw a new hotel glowing in the

distance. She closed her eyes. "Please, God, let there be a room. If not . . . we'll sleep in the car."

She parked, scooped Daniel into her arms, and approached the front desk.

"I need a room. Just for tonight."

The clerk tapped a few keys. "Would you prefer a single or a double?"

Relief washed over her like a wave. She handed him a credit card. "It doesn't matter."

He gave her a room key. A door. A moment of peace.

Chelsea opened the hotel door and collapsed onto the bed with her son. Daniel curled against her, his head nestled in the crook of her shoulder.

"I've got you," she whispered. "I'll always take care of you. I promise."

The temptation to give up tugged at her thoughts. It would be so easy to close her eyes and never wake up. But she pushed it aside. She couldn't fall apart—not now.

There were children counting on her.

She stared at the ceiling, thinking of her family, her friends, and the voices that warned her. The ones who would see her now and say, "Told you so."

But none of them knew what she had endured. None of them had seen the bruises on her soul.

She held Daniel close and kissed his forehead.

It had all started with a toast to dreams, to love, to forever.

Now, all she had left was survival.

How did my dreams turn into this nightmare? she thought, tears trailing silently down her cheeks. "How did I not see this coming?"

Her final thought before drifting into sleep was a whisper—raw, aching, and uncertain.

"How will I survive?"

And yet when she awoke the next morning, she realized she already had.

Chapter Two

All That's Left

Three years later

Chelsea lay stretched across the bed of her hotel room, the fireplace casting flickering shadows across the walls on this cold December afternoon. Her fingers hovered over her phone, debating whether to call or not. She'd played this moment over in her head a hundred times, but hesitation gripped her like frost on a windowpane.

Her best friend Maya lounged beside her, less patient and far more direct.

"Oh, come on, girl," Maya groaned, exasperated. "Can we please put an end to this drama? Just call him. You want to. I want you to. Let's both stop suffering already. I'm so tired of hearing you go in circles about this and not doing anything about it. What have you got to lose?"

Chelsea sighed. "It's not about losing, Maya. It's just . . . we haven't spoken in almost a week. One minute we're talking every day, and then, nothing. It's not like he's my boyfriend. I can't just call him out of nowhere and be like, 'Hey, what's up?'"

Maya sat up straighter, folding her arms. "You're not starting anything new. You've already been talking. So call and keep talking. It's a continuation, not a first move."

Chelsea frowned. "Still feels like I'm chasing. I've never chased anyone in my life. I hate how women throw themselves at men these days. I don't want to be lumped in with that."

"You?" Maya laughed. "Lumped in with *that*? Chels, please. You overanalyze *everything*. A rose can't even bloom around you without you questioning its origin, its meaning, and whether it's emotionally fulfilled. Let it just *be*. For once, let something just *be*."

Chelsea tried not to laugh, but Maya's dramatic hand gestures and head-shaking were hard to ignore.

"Besides," Maya continued, "you're the one who ended your last conversation early. You said you'd call him back. So technically, you're the one who ghosted."

Chelsea bit her lip. "You make it sound so easy."

"That's because it *is*. You're making it harder than it needs to be. Look, you and Tristen have been talking for weeks. He flirts. He gets all excited when you call him 'honey.' He even offered to drop everything and meet you in the city the day you had a meeting—no notice. That says something."

Chelsea nodded, still unconvinced.

"It's the week before Christmas," Maya added. "People are busy—shopping, visiting family. He could just be waiting for *you* to follow up. Don't turn this into a lifetime movie. It's just a call. That's it."

Chelsea sighed. "Alright. Maybe you're right."

"Thank you! It's settled. You make the call, and I'll go downstairs and finish sorting those boxes. After that, we'll head over to your new house and start unloading, then grab a bite. All this moving has me starving."

Left alone with her phone, Chelsea stared at the screen. Her fingers hovered, hesitated, then typed the number. At the final digit, she pressed "End Call."

Again.

What is this? she thought. Bold and confident in every other aspect of life, she suddenly felt like a schoolgirl. Ridiculous. She dialed again. And again, she canceled at the last second.

This time, she made herself a promise: *Dial all ten numbers. Leave a message if necessary. No turning back.*

Downstairs, Maya's voice rang through the suite. "Chelsea! I know you're still upstairs talking to yourself. If you don't call him in the next 2.3 seconds, I'm coming up there and doing it myself, and I will embarrass you. Try me!"

Chelsea let out a laugh and pressed "Call."

To her surprise, Tristen picked up.

"Hi, Tristen. It's Chelsea. How are you?"

His voice came through, warm and unmistakably pleased. "Hey, Chelsea. I'm good. How about you?"

She grinned, settling into the conversation. "Good. Deep in relocation mode."

"Did you close on your house yet?"

"Sure did! I'm staying at the Residence Inn for now. My best friend came from Virginia to help, and we've been shuffling boxes all weekend. Technically, I've got three places right now."

With a playful tone, Tristen said, "Oh yeah? Am I invited to the new one?"

Chelsea's stomach flipped. His voice always had that effect on her. Trying to keep her tone casual, she replied, "Possibly. But it might take me a minute to get the place set up."

"I'm low maintenance," he said. "We could have a picnic on the floor. I'll bring the food and the wine."

Chelsea froze for a beat. What should she say? Something clever? Something sexy? Was she even capable of sexy anymore?

"Hmmm . . ." she said, lowering her voice. "That might be fun. Just let me know when."

"I'll be back in town in seven days."

"I'll pencil you in."

"Pencil?" he teased. "No way. I want a permanent marker."

She laughed. "Is that right?"

"That's right."

His voice had a street edge to it that sent tingles through her. It reminded her of something raw and unfiltered. It made her nervous—in a good way.

They talked about her boys next—Daniel and Matthew were staying with her parents for the school year. With no kindergarten openings midyear and wanting to preserve Daniel's friendships and routine, Chelsea had made the difficult decision to let them stay behind until June.

"So, you're going to be without them for six months?" Tristen asked gently. "Are you going to be okay?"

"I don't know," she admitted. "This will be the first time in my life I'm away from them this long. But my parents are amazing, and the boys are in a familiar place. That makes it easier."

"If you ever feel lonely," he said, "remember, I'm just one town over."

Chelsea giggled.

When she asked where he was now, he said he was visiting his mother and grandmother in Atlanta. "I try to come down a few times a year."

"Aww," she teased. "Someone's a mama's boy."

"Nah. But I've got her back."

As their conversation deepened, the tone shifted—more flirtation, more trust, more ease.

He suddenly asked, "So . . . what took you so long to call?"

Chelsea deflected. "The phone works both ways."

"True. But if roles were reversed, you'd be trippin'."

She laughed. "Maybe."

They both knew the truth.

She confessed she'd been buried under work, seminary, and the demands of relocating. He shared that he'd been closing out the fiscal year himself. Their lives were hectic, but somehow this connection felt effortless.

Chelsea found herself smiling as she listened to him talk. Their rhythm felt natural, like old friends reuniting. She rarely let people in, but Tristen had slipped through the cracks. Her walls hadn't just fallen; they'd crumbled.

She remembered a prophet once telling her she'd built emotional walls so high they were protected by sharks and guarded by a drawbridge. It was true. After all she had endured, she couldn't afford to fall in love with the wrong man again. So she'd prayed. If she was ever to marry again, she wanted God to send her *the one*. No detours. No more heartbreak. And now, here was Tristen.

An hour passed before she finally said, "As much as I'd love to keep talking, I've got to run. Still a lot of moving to do. Plus, Maya's probably wondering if I've abandoned her."

"Understandable."

"If you need a ride from the airport next week, let me know. I'm only twenty minutes away."

"Appreciate that," he said. "Thanks for calling tonight. If you're free tomorrow, I'll call you."

She smiled so hard her cheeks hurt. "Sure, I'll be around."

"Cool."

"Goodnight, Tristen."

"Peace."

* * *

Tristen ended the call with a grin. He hadn't felt this way in a long time. There was something about Chelsea—her voice, her spirit, her realness. She wasn't like other women he'd dated. She was grounded. God-centered. Genuine. Yet approachable.

He'd grown up in the church, the son of a preacher. He had seen behind the pulpit and witnessed too much, especially that one moment that still haunted him.

He clenched his fists at the memory: twelve years old, hiding behind the curtain in his father's office, planning to surprise him. But *he* was the one who ended up surprised. Miss Phyllis— her lips on his father's—looked up, locked eyes with him, and did not stop. She stared straight at him, fully aware that *young Tristen* was watching... and kept right on kissing him.

That moment rewired him. Whatever dreams he'd had of ministry died right there. He began pulling away from everything it claimed to be.

Until now.

Until Chelsea.

"Only time will tell," he whispered. "But for now, I like the way you make my heart beat."

* * *

Back upstairs, Chelsea flung herself onto the bed with a giddy squeal.

"Maya!" she called. "I think I just met Mr. Right!"

Maya came running. "What in the world . . . ? Girl, slow down. Aren't you the same person who's always telling everyone not to fall too fast?"

"I didn't say I was in love."

Maya pointed at her. "You didn't *have* to. It's written all over your face."

Chelsea laughed. "Okay, okay. But I haven't felt like this in *so* long. I actually *like* someone again. It feels . . . amazing."

They gathered their things and headed to a restaurant near Chelsea's new house. Over dinner and a round of celebratory mudslides, they reflected on the whirlwind year: a promotion into management, acceptance into seminary, the purchase of her new home—and now, maybe, just maybe, the beginning of something new.

But as the drinks arrived and Chelsea bowed her head to pray, a strange stillness came over her.

When she looked up, her face was serious. "Maya, I don't think I should be drinking this."

Maya blinked. "Why? Is something wrong with it?"

"No. It's not the drink. It's . . . me. I've been struggling with this for a while. Every sermon I hear lately seems to mention alcohol. I wonder if God is nudging me to give it up—maybe as part of my ministry."

Maya looked at her for a moment, then gently pushed Chelsea's glass toward herself. "If that's how you feel, then honor it. And don't worry—I'll take care of this poor, unwanted drink. There are starving people out there, and I'd hate to see it go to waste."

Chelsea laughed, but she knew Maya was right. If God was asking something of her, she wanted to obey.

She lifted her water glass. Maya mirrored her with a wink.

"To a beautiful new year," Maya said. "If how this one ended is any sign of what's ahead, you're in for something extraordinary."

Chapter Three

When the Mirror Breaks

Three years later

Chelsea stood tall in a black-and-white pinstriped suit, her long brown hair cascading over her shoulders. The boardroom quieted as she gathered her notes and addressed her team.

"Alright, everyone, this has been a very productive meeting," she began. "I'll follow up with the VPs to confirm their commitment to the project plan and create the communication we'll send to the field organization. Lynette, please reach out to the Training and Development team to determine the timeline for building the web design we discussed. Also, ask if they can recommend any external vendors to help expedite the process."

She paused before continuing.

"Brice, gather the necessary HR documentation to upload into the system. I'll assemble a team to test the platform's functionality. I'll also circulate a summary of today's action items, including timelines, to ensure we're all aligned. Let's reconvene in one week to review progress. Any questions or comments before we wrap?"

Tim lifted his head, a smug expression settling across his face. His piercing blue eyes met Chelsea's, and the crooked grin forming at the corners of his mouth warned her that a challenge was coming.

Clearing his throat, he said, "Chelsea, I know you're relatively new to the home office and not exactly from an IT background, so this might not make sense to you, but don't you think we're missing a huge opportunity by not using this project to update the field's call reporting system?"

Chelsea offered him a calm smile. She gently tucked a strand of hair behind her ear, pausing for a moment. Then, she met his gaze directly. "I can understand why you'd want to leverage this project for a system upgrade, especially given your passion for emerging tech."

Tim shifted uncomfortably in his seat as Chelsea stepped closer, her tone still measured.

"With your background, I imagine watching the field use what seems like outdated software must be frustrating." She moved behind him and rested a hand lightly on his shoulder. "I don't claim to be an IT expert, Tim. But I do have over a decade of field sales and management experience. And if there's one thing I know for sure, it's that the field dreads system changes. Some reps are still struggling to adjust to the last upgrade—two years ago."

Lynette chimed in, exasperated, "I can confirm that. I still get weekly calls from managers asking why we couldn't just leave the old system alone. It's like they're allergic to change."

Chelsea nodded and returned to the front of the room. "And more importantly, Tim, the kind of change you're suggesting isn't within our project scope." She glanced around the table. "We need to remain disciplined about scope. When new ideas pop into our heads, we have to revisit the original framework. If it doesn't fit, it stays off the table. Otherwise, we risk project creep—taking on too much, losing focus, and compromising our core objectives. Make sense?"

Heads around the table nodded.

"Yes, ma'am," Calvin added.

Tim raised his hands in resignation, clearly conceding. "Alright. I just don't get why the field folks always resist simple upgrades. It's bizarre."

Chelsea smiled. "Every team has its quirks. But let's not forget—it's our salespeople who drive revenue and keep us all employed. That's worth remembering." She glanced at the room. "If there are no further questions, we're done here. Great work, team."

As the group dispersed, Lynette approached Chelsea and tugged gently at her arm. "I have to admit, I was skeptical about this project. It felt too big to pull off on such a tight timeline, but it's coming together beautifully. This system is going to be amazing."

Chelsea's face brightened. "Thanks, Lynette. Everyone's been putting in the work. Believe it or not, we're ahead of schedule."

Lynette gasped. "Ahead? That's a first for me. If this keeps up, my department could save over a hundred thousand dollars. I might even get a raise." She folded her arms and leaned in, lowering her voice. "Honestly, I didn't think someone as young as you could pull this off. Managing all these personalities? No, thank you. Especially Tim—he thinks he can say anything he wants because his father's a big deal around here. And don't get me started on the women in his department feeding that overblown ego."

Chelsea suppressed a grimace. Lynette's tuna-scented breath, paired with a poppy seed lodged between her front teeth, made her stomach churn.

"Well, he does bring some strong ideas to the table," Chelsea offered diplomatically.

"I guess," Lynette said with a shrug. "But still, you've got this unique way of motivating people and getting everyone on board. I'm impressed."

"Thanks . . . I think." Chelsea smiled. "I've got to get back to my desk and fire off a few emails before heading home. I've got a hot date with my boys tonight."

"See you next week!"

As Chelsea walked toward her office, she heard rapid footsteps behind her.

"Chelsea! Mind if I walk back with you?"

She turned to see her boss, John, flushed and slightly winded.

"Not if you're planning a sprint," she teased. "Unlike you, I'm in three-inch heels."

He glanced at her shoes and chuckled. "Fair enough. I'll slow down."

"So, what's up?" she asked.

"Just wanted to say how well you handled that meeting. I came to observe progress on the systems project, and I've got to say, you're making it look easy. Great leadership, kiddo. I'm late for a call, but let's catch up tomorrow. I need to hand off a few projects your way. Maybe we can grab lunch?"

"Sounds good," she replied.

As John hurried ahead, Chelsea's smile faded. His "kiddo" comment lingered, echoing her old insecurities. It was the second time that day someone had referenced her age, and it brought her back to the beginning of her career.

At twenty-one, she'd been the youngest in her company. Her age had felt like a target on her back—something people resented rather than respected. Even when her performance excelled, people dismissed her ideas or used her youth to block her progress.

She remembered Amy, the manager who always found a reason to hold her back. "You're young, Chelsea. You've got time," she would say as she passed her over for promotion—again and again. It chipped away at her confidence until she vowed never to broadcast her age again. At Drake Pharmaceuticals, she kept that part of herself guarded. But every now and then—like today—it came back to sting.

Chelsea returned to her office, booted up her computer, and began tackling the forty-three emails that had piled up in the last two hours. After flying through thirty-one responses, she glanced at the clock.

She was late.

Quickly shutting down, she packed her belongings. Today wasn't just another Tuesday—it was her thirtieth birthday. She had promised her sons she would be home early, and she intended to keep that promise.

As she walked to the parking garage, her thoughts swirled.

Thirty. I made it. But I thought it would look so different.

She climbed into her car and searched for a station to lift her mood. Her fingers landed on one playing an oldie but goodie— Donald Lawrence.

"It's a New Season," she read on her dashboard. "Perfect."

She cranked the volume and began to jam.

"It's a new season . . . It's a new day . . . Fresh anointing coming my way . . ." Singing loudly, she waved her hands in the air, clapping and bouncing in her seat. "Go Chelsea, go Chelsea—it's your birthday!"

Her phone rang.

"Aw man, who's killing my vibe?" she muttered, fumbling through her purse to find her phone. Swerving back into her lane, she answered.

"Hello?"

"Happy birthday to you!" Nicky's familiar voice sang from the other end. "How old are you now? Wait—should I not ask? You get weird about that, remember?"

"Girl, please," Chelsea laughed. "You can ask. I just don't tell the people at work. But yes, today I am officially the big three-zero!"

"How does it feel to hit thirty?"

"To be honest?" Chelsea sighed. "A little depressing. I've been divorced for seven years, still single. No husband in sight."

Nicky laughed gently. "At least you're only thirty. I'm thirty-eight and in the same boat."

"You're not helping."

"Look at the bright side. We've got kids already, so there's no ticking clock. Although . . ." Chelsea trailed off. "I thought I'd have one more by now."

"You still could. You're young."

"Maybe. But the older I get, the less I want bottles and diapers. Matthew and Daniel are independent now. I don't know if I want to start all over again."

Suddenly, Chelsea gasped. "Shoot—I missed my exit!"

"You better focus," Nicky warned. "Call me later."

"No, I'm good. Already turned around. But I do feel guilty for being down."

"Why?"

"Because when I left work today, I thought about how far I've come. Seven years ago, my life was a disaster. I was broke, working two jobs, barely surviving. And now . . . look what God has done. I have no right to complain."

Nicky agreed. "You should be celebrating. You have a beautiful home, two amazing kids, and you're killing it at work.

Girl, you even have groupies."

"Oh, please. You're the one who knows everyone."

Chelsea grew quiet. "Nick, can I be honest? When I left Lythicom, I was in a dark place. They treated me poorly. My manager blocked my promotions and belittled me at every opportunity. I was told that my looks, my age, and even my divorce made me a liability."

She paused, emotion rising in her throat.

"To make ends meet, I waited tables at night. I was exhausted—barely sleeping, raising two kids, dodging coworkers in restaurants so they wouldn't see me bussing tables. I felt humiliated. But I kept praying. And then one day, a recruiter from Drake called out of the blue."

She smiled at the memory.

"Within thirty days, I got the job. They gave me a 50 percent raise. And within eighteen months, I was promoted to management—with another raise. By twenty-six, I was one of the youngest district managers in the company's history."

"That's incredible."

"It was God," Chelsea whispered. "I didn't chase the promotion. It found me. And the interview? We ended up talking about faith. That's when I knew—I was supposed to be there." She paused again. "Sometimes, I think God lets us get uncomfortable so we're finally willing to move."

Nicky sighed. "That's my life. I had to catch Martin in bed with another woman before I finally left. And, girl, yes, I grabbed a frying pan."

Chelsea burst out laughing. "A frying pan?"

"Yes! A cast-iron one! That tramp ran out of my house naked."

"Oh my goodness!" Chelsea wheezed between laughs. "You never told me all that!"

"Girl, it's funny now, but I almost lost my mind that day. The betrayal, the humiliation . . . But it forced me to walk away. Just like your mess pushed you into your miracle."

Chelsea nodded. "Exactly."

"Alright," Nicky said. "Finish your story. How'd you leave Lythicom?"

"I told you about the recruiter. He said someone recommended me. I still don't know who. But within a month, I had the offer. Giving my resignation was one of the best moments of my life. And here I am: new city, new role, quadrupled salary, new home."

"Chelsea, after everything you've just said, how can you be sad about turning thirty?"

"You're right," Chelsea said. "I've got a lot to celebrate."

She pulled into the school parking lot. "I've got to go get the boys. It's five fifty-nine, and pickup is at six."

"Enjoy your birthday, girl. You've earned it."

Chelsea hung up and walked into the building. She spotted her sons from across the room. "Daniel, Matthew, let's go!"

They ran to their lockers and gathered their things. "Hi, Mom!" they shouted.

Matthew hugged her tightly. Daniel gave her a high five.

"You promised you'd be early!" Matthew scolded.

"I know, baby. Mommy got a little turned around."

Daniel raised an eyebrow. "Lost? You come home every day. Not the brightest crayon in the box, huh?"

"Watch your mouth," Chelsea laughed. "That's my line."

"Nuh-uh. I get my brains from Dad!"

"Whatever," she said, laughing. "Come on. Let's get dinner."

"Can we stop by the house first?" Matthew asked, a sly smile on his face.

"Why?"

"Maybe we have a surprise . . ."

She rolled her eyes, pretending to protest. "Fine. But it has to be quick. And then dinner—my choice."

Daniel nodded. "Fair. It's your birthday."

Chelsea smiled. For once, her desires came first—and that, in itself, was a gift.

Chapter Four

The Weight of Almost

"Alright, we're home," Chelsea announced as she pulled into the driveway. "But this is just a quick stop, okay? Run inside, grab what you need, use the bathroom, and we're back out. Got it?"

She knew herself too well. If she stayed in the house longer than five minutes, the comfort of home would sink into her bones, and she wouldn't want to leave again. As she slipped her key into the door, she noticed the hallway light shining from inside.

"Daniel? Matthew? Did one of you leave the light on again? Do you know how high the electricity bill is? Every time you leave a light on, it costs Mommy a lot of money."

"But, Mommy," Matthew said innocently, "you can just go to the bank and get more."

Chelsea sighed. "How many times do I have to explain this? I wish it were that easy, but money doesn't grow on trees. Please be more careful."

Matthew, never one to miss an opportunity, quickly replied, "Yes, it does. Paper comes from trees, and money is made from paper, so money *does* grow on trees."

Chelsea laughed. "Alright, smart guy. Try taking a piece of tree bark into the store and see if they let you buy candy with it. When they throw you out, come tell me how much money we have growing in our backyard."

With a final turn of the knob, the door opened. Chelsea stepped inside and froze. Standing in the entryway were her parents.

"Mom? Dad? What are you doing here? When did you— how did you . . . ?"

She was too shocked to finish a single sentence. Her parents had moved to a retirement community in North Carolina two months ago. She hadn't expected to see them in person for quite some time.

Her father smiled warmly. "You didn't think we'd miss your thirtieth birthday, did you?"

"We flew in this morning," her mother added. "Just in time to straighten up a bit around here."

Her mother never missed a chance to drop hints about tidiness. In her eyes, a clean home was essential to landing a husband—and Chelsea, now thirty and seven years divorced, was apparently on borrowed time.

Not that Chelsea didn't want to get married again. It just wasn't that simple. She couldn't bring herself to waste energy on someone she didn't see a future with. Her mother didn't know the truth—that Chelsea still carried feelings for the only man she had seriously dated since her divorce. Even after two years, Tristen remained lodged in her heart.

She often wondered why she couldn't let him go. Why hadn't the memory of his betrayal faded? Why, after all the hurt, did she still love him?

She remembered his mesmerizing eyes and the way he looked at her—like she was his whole world. When he was in a romantic mood, he would brush her hair gently and sing to her, always ending with her wrapped in his arms. He had an indescribable charm that made everyone gravitate toward him—especially her.

Tristen had a rare blend of confidence and vulnerability. He was grounded but could navigate any circle—whether a room full of Ivy League professionals or kids from the block. That made him irresistible to women, but it was Chelsea who had his heart.

He wasn't perfect. He wasn't even traditionally handsome. But somehow, when all his qualities came together, he was unforgettable. He made her laugh, made her feel beautiful, encouraged her dreams, and calmed her anxieties. Yet he shattered her. Completely.

Even thinking about it pulled her toward a place she didn't want to revisit. How had she gotten so close to committing to forever, only for it to fall apart in a single moment? All the good times, the bad, the promises—gone. And still, the love remained.

As her parents stood in the doorway, smiling, Chelsea's mind drifted back to the very first time she spoke to Tristen, nearly five years ago. It was three years after her divorce from Collin, just after she had been promoted to district manager.

A colleague had suggested she reach out to his brother at headquarters—Tristen. Curious and open to new connections, she made the call. From that first conversation, she felt something stir. It had been so long since she had felt anything romantic that the sensation was almost foreign.

Tristen was sharp, witty, and spiritual, with a raw, streetwise edge that both intrigued and disarmed her. It was a dangerous combination for Chelsea, and one she found impossible to resist. He seemed practiced in charm, yet there was something guarded about him—as if he carried secrets buried just beneath the surface.

They spoke for an hour that night. She teased him about running from God—and maybe from himself. Her intuition told her he was hiding something. Over time, she would learn just how right she had been.

Their phone calls stretched across weeks. The more they talked, the more she felt drawn in. Coincidentally, after her relocation, she discovered she had moved just a town away from him. Fate, perhaps?

Eventually, they agreed to meet. She had a meeting at the home office where he worked, and they arranged to have lunch. Since she didn't know the area, he offered to meet her partway and let her follow him in.

Their first meeting was set for a McDonald's about twenty miles from the office. That morning, Chelsea spent over an hour digging through her closet. Black? Always classy. Red? Bold and striking. Nothing felt right—until she found a brick-red sweater and a black skirt. With knee-high boots and a belt, the look came together. She added red lipstick and a black leather coat to complete the ensemble.

She looked stunning.

But she hadn't heard from Tristen all morning. He had a tendency to go off the grid, and although they spoke almost daily, he could be frustratingly unreliable. Still, she reminded herself—they weren't "official." Just friends. Maybe more.

Her heart pounded with anticipation and nerves. He was the first man she'd been drawn to since her divorce. Could he be the one? She had prayed so often: *God, don't send me more dates. Just send me my husband, and I'll wait.* But waiting wasn't easy.

Time ticked by. She called him repeatedly. No answer. Just when discouragement threatened to take over, he called.

"What's going on, babe?"

"What do you mean, 'What's going on'? Weren't we supposed to meet?"

"Oh man, I totally forgot. I haven't even gotten dressed yet."

Chelsea sighed. "I can't believe this. I needed you to guide me to the office."

"Alright, alright. Give me a minute. Take exit 42. There's a McDonald's about a mile down on the right. Wait there. I'll be there in about thirty minutes."

Frustrated but relieved, Chelsea parked and went inside. She ordered coffee and opened her laptop to get some work done while she waited. Her thoughts drifted. What if he wasn't as attractive in person as he was on the phone? What if the chemistry wasn't there when they met? Was she doing the right thing?

Just then, she heard someone call her name.

She turned slowly, hoping to conceal any immediate reaction.

It was Tristen.

"Wow . . . you are beautiful," he said sincerely.

Chelsea smiled, while her inner voice winced. *Why is he wearing that awful denim shirt with black dress pants?*

Still, she found his eyes captivating—eyes that seemed to hold entire stories. She stared into them, hoping for answers, a glimpse of truth.

He dropped his gaze.

"Why won't you look at me?" she asked.

"Because I feel like you can see right through me," he replied.

"Do you have something to hide?"

"Don't we all?" he said softly. "Stop looking at me like that. You're going to say you have a prophetic word for me, aren't you? People have been telling me for years who I'm supposed to be and what God wants from me. It never ends."

Chelsea leaned in. "You don't have to receive everything others say. Prophetic words usually confirm what God has already placed in your spirit. My question is—what are *you* running from?"

He cut her off. "We're going to be late. We should go."

Chelsea nodded. "Fine. But you know, Tristen, eventually you'll have to face whatever you're running from."

She had no idea how true her words would become. Tristen's hidden truths would surface one day, and with them, they would unravel her world.

As she followed him out of the restaurant, Chelsea felt a whirlwind of emotions. Curiosity. Excitement. Fear. The chemistry between them was undeniable, but so was the mystery. He was open yet closed. Transparent yet hidden. She felt compelled to uncover his depths.

She had no idea that once she did, she'd wish she never had.

Drawn to Fire

Chelsea sat at a bustling dinner table with her children and parents, reflecting on the last few years of her life while Daniel and Matthew tried to coax their grandparents into revealing her age.

After several failed attempts, Matthew pouted and said, "Come on, Mom. When are you going to spill it? Didn't you tell us you're not supposed to keep secrets in a family?"

Chelsea smirked. "Yes, but this isn't a secret. It's just none of your business. You'll understand when it's time to know."

"Mom, that doesn't make sense," Daniel countered.

Chelsea straightened in her chair and placed her hands on her waist. "See? You're too young to get it, but it makes perfect sense to me. That's why you can't handle how old I am. Now, how was school today?"

She often steered conversations in new directions when they veered toward uncomfortable topics. It usually worked, though she suspected her window was closing, especially with Daniel. He was growing wiser to her ways with each passing day.

Daniel, in many ways, was an old soul in a young boy's body. His maturity frequently caught people off guard. Chelsea sometimes wondered whether witnessing the collapse of her marriage had imprinted something heavy on him. Unlike Matthew—carefree, lively, and largely indifferent to his parents' romantic history—Daniel harbored hope that his family might one day be whole again. His quiet mission to reunite his parents surfaced often, sometimes at the most inconvenient moments.

Matthew spoke up again, still frowning. "My day was okay, but Brian Silverman kept picking his nose and trying to wipe his boogers on me."

Chelsea closed her eyes and covered her ears. Her body cringed. "Gross! I'm trying to eat here!"

Matthew giggled. "They were green and yellow, and he was farting too!"

With both hands over her face now, Chelsea shouted, "Enough!"

Matthew nearly fell out of his chair laughing. "You asked!"

"Not about that."

"Mommy, why didn't you invite Daddy to celebrate with us?" Daniel asked abruptly.

Chelsea sighed. Here we go again. "We've talked about this, Daniel. Your father and I are divorced. It wouldn't be appropriate for him to celebrate my birthday with me."

"But aren't you guys friends? And don't friends celebrate birthdays together?" Matthew chimed in.

"We're friendly because we co-parent you two, not because we're best buddies. Capisce?"

"Capisce?" asked Matthew, mispronouncing the word.

"That means: do you understand?"

"Oh . . . well, why didn't you just say that?"

"Because I didn't. I'm expanding your vocabulary. Now, did you two wash your hands before diving into that bread?"

Both boys looked guilty. "No," they answered in unison.

Chelsea stood. "Let's go. Time to wash those hands, jelly beans."

Peter offered, "Do you want me to take them, honey?"

"It's okay, Dad. You and Mom had a long day of travel. Relax. We'll be right back."

As Chelsea led the boys away, Lynda leaned toward her husband. "That was a close call."

Peter looked puzzled. "What do you mean?"

"Didn't you notice Daniel was about to bring up Chelsea

and Collin again? He's still feeding those boys hope that they'll reunite. I'm surprised he didn't ask them to get her to invite him tonight. That boy is holding on."

Peter's voice softened. "It's hard for a man to let go of a woman he still loves. You know that."

Lynda rubbed his leg affectionately. "I know, but it's like he forgot the pain he caused. My blood still boils when I think about what happened in that house. Chelsea never told us everything, but I'll never forget the sound of her voice that night she called. She tried to sound like it was no big deal, but I could hear through her strength. When she walked through our door—God, she looked like she hadn't slept in days. That's when I knew it was serious."

Peter nodded. "I saw it too. She avoided eye contact with me that first day. Chelsea always smiles to cover the hurt."

"In some ways, I was more worried about Collin," Peter admitted. "He looked shattered. Losing your family—especially like that—changes a man. He was a kid who made some terrible mistakes and paid dearly."

Lynda narrowed her eyes. "Are you saying you want them back together?"

"No. I'm saying they were young, and mistakes were made. But I won't deny he loved her."

"Maybe. But he had a terrible way of showing it."

Peter nodded. "Perhaps he never learned how to love. Losing his mother at five left a hole. When we first met him, he couldn't even hug me without discomfort."

"And then his father remarried that Sophia woman only six months later. Poor Collin never stood a chance."

Peter chuckled. "A six-foot-tall correctional officer would

scare anyone."

"I'm not joking. She tore into everyone—especially Collin. That last time they visited, I nearly lost it. She walked in, looked around like she was taking inventory, and started with those little comments... the kind that sound polite but aren't. The house, the way I had things set up—nothing quite measured up.

Right there in the living room, in front of everyone—she kept interrupting him, correcting little things, finishing his sentences like he couldn't get it right on his own. He tried to laugh it off, but you could see it land. Little by little. You could feel the air shift."

"Chelsea noticed, too. I wonder if she still had feelings for him then."

"She was still recovering from the divorce. It was raw. She had just had Matthew. Everything was fragile, and she was trying to keep the peace."

Peter agreed. "And maybe Collin was trying to prove he could change. He held his tongue, probably to show Chelsea he'd grown."

"Maybe. I nudged him under the table that night, trying to give him some strength. But I swore never to invite Sophia over again. How his father tolerates her is beyond me."

Peter shrugged. "Twenty years of marriage might've numbed him."

Lynda folded her arms. "There's no excuse for allowing your wife to tear down your child. Collin paid the price, and so did Chelsea. I don't know how she got into that mess. She had everything going for her."

Chelsea returned with the boys, and Lynda abruptly ended the conversation.

Peter smiled at them. "Finally decided to rejoin us, huh? We thought you got lost."

Chelsea glanced at her parents. Their expressions told her everything. They had been talking about her. She forced a smile. "Apparently, Matthew needed more than just handwashing."

Lynda beamed at her daughter as she sat down. No matter what life threw at her, Chelsea always found a way to stand strong. Her resilience astounded Lynda—even if she didn't always understand her daughter's choices.

Still, Lynda couldn't help but reflect on the past. Chelsea's strength reminded her of what she once longed for. What if she had taken the risks Chelsea took? Gone back to school? Started her own business? Chased her buried dreams?

Matthew pulled her from her thoughts. "Grandma, what are you thinking about? Your face looks not-fun. It's Mommy's birthday. Smile, Nana."

Lynda laughed. "I was just thinking about how good God is. I never knew how much joy grandchildren would bring."

Matthew smiled. "We're special, aren't we, Nana? And so are you—and Mommy and Poppy and Auntie and Vince and . . ."

Chelsea looked at her mother and instantly understood the thoughts behind her eyes. She didn't let it bother her. Her mother was proud of her now, but she would always wonder what life could've been if she had taken a different path. What her mother didn't realize was that Chelsea often wondered the same thing.

Chapter Six

A Glimpse into His Shadows

J ust as Chelsea put her pen down and prepared to turn in for the night, her phone rang.

"Hello?"

"Hi, Chelsea. It's Collin. I just wanted to wish you a happy thirtieth birthday, old lady."

She chuckled. "So nice of you to remember."

"How could I forget? We *were* married, you know. So . . . how was your day?"

"It was okay. My parents surprised me. They flew in to spend the week with me, and we all had a great dinner. It's always nice having them around."

"I bet. Now you don't have to cook for a week."

Laughing, she replied, "Exactly. You know I'm always happy to hand my kitchen over to my mom."

"Yeah, I remember. You weren't too shy about sending me in there either. But that's probably because I can cook better than you."

"Please, Collin. You know I taught you everything you know. Stop spreading lies to Daniel and Matthew, telling them you're the better cook."

"I don't tell them that. They've just figured it out for themselves. Smart boys."

They laughed together, the ease between them a surprising contrast to the years of strain they had weathered. After fifteen minutes of conversation, filled with light teasing and weekend plans for the boys, they said their goodbyes.

* * *

Collin hung up the phone and sat in silence, a dull ache rising in his chest. Would he and Chelsea ever find their way back to each other? He knew he had made mistakes, but she wasn't blameless either.

He closed his eyes, trying to remember what it felt like to hold her in his arms.

God, will I have to pay forever for the mistakes I made? he thought.

He shook his head slowly, sighing deeply.

I moved away from my family so we could be close to hers. I found a decent job. I didn't abandon my responsibilities like so many others might have. And still, look how it ended.

He thought of the little things—the candles, the flowers, the late-night efforts to rekindle intimacy. He had tried to express his love, but somehow, it had never been enough. When she left, everything unraveled. He had never felt so empty. She had been the one person in his life he had opened up to, and then she was gone.

He had never imagined she would actually leave. He might have threatened her in anger, but he would never have walked away. He even joined the Catholic Church for her—only for her to later convert to Protestantism. When she immersed herself in her new church, spending hours there, he grew resentful. His silent punishment was to withdraw—emotionally and verbally.

Eventually, he turned to alcohol.

Why did I let it get this far? he asked himself. *Why didn't I suggest counseling? Talk things through? The Hennessy numbed the pain, but it never filled the void.*

When she left, it felt like a part of him had died. He lost his house, his family, his pride—and almost his job. He hated her. Or maybe he hated what he had become. Oddly, the only people who showed him compassion were her parents. They would sit with him for hours, listening as he poured out his regret.

He remembered leaving notes for Chelsea, calling her, hoping to pull her back in. It had worked once before—but not this time.

Collin bowed his head.

God, thank You for pulling me out of that darkness. Thank You for helping me get back on my feet. If there's any chance left, please help Chelsea and me find our way back to each other. I believe she still loves me deep down. Soften her heart. Help her forgive. We've come so far. Maybe one day . . . maybe we can try again. Amen.

He turned off the light, his mind drifting to the day he had finally asked her out again. She had declined, gently but firmly, saying their friendship was more valuable than risking another heartbreak. She reminded him of how far they'd come—from restraining orders to co-parenting amicably.

How could you ever think I'd want to hurt you? he thought bitterly. *I may have let my anger get the best of me . . . I may have thrown things at you and said things I wish I could take back, but I did love you. I still do.*

But she wasn't wearing a ring. Not yet. So there was still hope.

* * *

When Chelsea hung up, she too sat in quiet reflection.

Look how far we've come, she thought.

Just a few years ago, they couldn't even have a conversation without screaming. She recalled how he had refused to sign the divorce papers, insisting that he couldn't live without her. He even tried to win her back with gifts, church visits, and emotional appeals. Once, he told her he had taken out a million-dollar life insurance policy in her name—"so it would behoove you to stay," he said.

It had been such a painful time. Pregnant, exhausted, and with nowhere else to go, she had returned to her parents' home. In desperation, she told Collin he could keep everything—the house, furniture, whatever—if he would just sign the papers and let her go.

He finally did, realizing he could no longer afford the house on his own. Chelsea bought it back, shouldering the mortgage and removing his name from the deed. But she hadn't anticipated how hard it would be.

Finances were tight. Her income barely covered essentials. Collin initially refused to pay child support, and resentment seemed to radiate from him like heat. He hated seeing her survive—and perhaps thrive—without him.

She remembered pleading with the bank for a loan, trying to keep the house afloat. There wasn't enough equity, and selling would mean taking a loss. Still, she managed. Somehow, by God's grace, she managed.

But moving back in wasn't the end of her troubles. The house needed repairs. She had no savings. And worst of all, women began calling the house, asking for Collin.

Had he really moved on that quickly? Or had he never truly been faithful?

She sighed, turning over in bed.

Raising two young children alone while working a demanding job—it was almost unbearable. She remembered the sleep deprivation, the emotional fatigue, the loneliness. Daniel drained her energy during the day, and Matthew kept her up all night. She was constantly on edge, sometimes falling asleep at the wheel.

Work wasn't a refuge either. A new colleague—an older man—seemed offended that she, a young woman, held the same title. He made her life miserable, spreading lies and undermining her.

Still, she smiled through it all. She told herself, *Life is a stage—play your part.*

But the math no longer added up. She needed more income. So, she humbled herself and took a night job as a waitress.

She had never asked for financial help. Not now. Not ever. She started working at fourteen and had never stopped. The thought of running into someone she knew while waiting tables was terrifying. And, of course, it happened. Colleagues came in. She ducked. She begged coworkers to take her tables. Then she'd go home at 11:00 p.m., pick up the kids, and do it all again the next day.

It was not the life she had dreamed of. Not by a long shot. To make matters worse, Collin seemed determined to punish her. He'd drop the boys off on the porch—barefoot, with suitcases, in their underwear. Sometimes they came home with unexplained cuts. Sometimes other women had cared for them. He took them to inappropriate movies.

Once, when picking them up, he refused to step inside. Chelsea handed the boys their breakfast in to-go containers. Collin made them sit on the porch and eat—like animals. When she objected, he pushed the food through the door and left.

She sobbed that day. How had it come to this?

But they were no longer in that place. Not anymore.

Chelsea sat up and whispered, "God, thank You. Thank You

for peace. We're not perfect, but we've come so far. If not for your grace, I would've lost my mind."

Smiling through tears, she rose from bed and knelt to pray.

Thank You for letting me make it to thirty. There were days I didn't think I'd live to see it. But I did. By your hand, I did. I just wish I weren't so alone.

She paused, her heart aching.

Tristen, she thought.

Everything changed with Tristen.

Chapter Seven

The Ties That Fray

At 5:15 a.m., Chelsea's alarm clock began beeping. Half-asleep, she reached over and slapped the snooze button. "Just five more minutes," she whispered, trying to negotiate with God as her Bible and journal sat patiently on her nightstand. She knew she needed to get up for her morning devotional, but the weight of another day pinned her to the mattress.

"I am so tired of my life," she murmured.

Another sixteen-hour day loomed—management meetings out of state, seminary class two hours away, a paper due next week, and barely any time left to spend with her boys or her visiting parents. She tried to remember if the kids had practice or tutoring today. The days blurred together.

Dragging herself out of bed, she splashed cold water on her face and tried to mentally organize her day.

"God, I am so tired, and the day hasn't even begun."

She was exhausted—physically, spiritually, emotionally. The endless juggling act between work, ministry, school, and motherhood left nothing for herself. Her greatest indulgence these days was a nap.

She stood in front of the mirror, brushing her teeth, when her mind drifted to the painful, hollow ache she couldn't seem to shake.

Tristen.

It had been over a year and a half, and her heart still ached when she thought of him.

"Damn you, Tristen. Damn you," she whispered.

The breakup still played in her mind like an unfinished film. She had told herself she wouldn't revisit that memory, but today, it barged in.

We were supposed to be married by now.

She touched her stomach. They had talked about having a child together. Would her womb ever know life again?

It had been nearly two years since Tristen had broken the news of his cancer diagnosis. That night had changed everything. He called her sobbing, unable to get the words out. Chelsea had pulled over, stepped out of the car so her kids wouldn't hear, and listened in horror as he whispered, "Chelsea . . . I have prostate cancer."

The words hit her like a sledgehammer. In that moment, she knew she couldn't let him face this alone—not that night. Once the boys were home, she made arrangements for a sitter, packed a small bag, and drove across multiple states to be with him.

When she arrived, he greeted her with a blank stare, then collapsed in her arms. They sat in a dark corner for hours. He'd confessed everything—his past, his mistakes, his shame. He'd believed his illness was punishment. Chelsea held his face, praying over him, whispering, "God still loves you. And so do I."

From that night forward, Chelsea never left his side—whether physically or virtually. She became his lifeline through scans, radiation, rectal bleeding, ulcers, surgery, and the depression that gripped him tightly. He hadn't told his family; she had become his secret keeper, his strength.

But then, one year later, things began to change.

Her thoughts drifted back to that fateful call the night before Christmas. Tristen's voice was low and weary.

"Baby, I'm tired of living like this," he had said. "I wake up five times a night. Sometimes I piss blood. Chelsea . . . I don't know how much longer I can do this."

She remembered offering to fly to Atlanta to see him. He had said no, but she heard something in his voice—something fragile, something final. She made up her mind that night.

She would fly to him. Surprise him. Pull him out of the dark.

When she landed in Atlanta, a warm-faced cab driver named David picked her up.

"Where to, miss?" he asked kindly.

Chelsea smiled. "I'm surprising my boyfriend. He's been going through a lot, and I just felt like he needed someone to show up for him."

David gave her a wary look in the rearview mirror. "Surprise? Hmm, I see this before. Maybe no good. You sure this is what you want to do?"

"I appreciate the concern," Chelsea said, "but he's not the cheating type. He's just been down. I think he'll be happy."

David hesitated, then handed her a card. "Take my number. Just in case. If you need ride, you call. I come."

Chelsea thanked him. As they pulled up to Tristen's building, she had an idea. "David, would you mind helping me surprise him? Could you ring the doorbell and say you have a delivery? That way, he won't know it's me."

David looked even more uneasy than before, his brows furrowed deeply. "Okay, miss. But . . . please be careful. I see things like this. Sometimes, surprise is not good."

A chill ran through her, but she shook it off. "Thank you, David. I'll be fine."

David walked up to the intercom and rang the buzzer. "Delivery," he said flatly. Tristen buzzed him in.

Chelsea climbed the stairs and knocked on the door. When Tristen opened it and saw her, his face flashed confusion, joy, and panic.

"What are you doing here?"

Chelsea smiled. "You sounded so low last night. I thought you could use an urgent pick-me-up."

"You shouldn't have come," he muttered, his tone clipped.

She laughed, brushing it aside. "I just wanted to see you. To remind you that you're not alone."

He asked her to wait outside while he tidied up. She could hear frantic rustling inside—bottles clinking, drawers slamming.

When she stepped inside, something felt off. He looked different. Walked differently. Talked differently. There was a heaviness in the air.

"You look like an angel in white," he said. "I don't want you to see me like this."

"If we're going to get married, it shouldn't matter how we look, should it? You still look like my Tristen."

His eyes welled with tears. "I was supposed to go to a black-tie event tonight. I can't believe you came."

"Go ahead. I'll be here when you get back."

"You shouldn't have come," he snapped again, pacing.

"Tristen, what is going on? Why are you acting like this?"

"I can't do this anymore, Chelsea. I just can't."

Her heart cracked. "I left my kids the day after Christmas for you. I thought you needed me."

He closed his eyes. "I do. But it's too much. I'm too much. I'm a mess. You deserve better."

"Stop it. I've stood by you through everything. I carried your secret when no one else knew. I've prayed, fasted, and believed with you. Why now? Why push me away now?"

He looked at her with pained eyes. "I told you not to come. You didn't listen."

Chelsea stepped forward, her voice trembling. "Can't do

what anymore, Tristen? What are you talking about?"

He exhaled sharply, turning away. "Us. I can't do us anymore. I'm not in the right place to be in a relationship. Not like this. Not now."

Chelsea blinked, stunned. The room felt like it was spinning.

"I don't want you seeing me like this. I don't even feel like a man anymore—half a man on my best day. And I can't have you seeing me like that. Not when I'm still fighting my way out."

She shook her head, tears threatening to fall. "If I leave now, I'm not coming back. I'm done. I told you a long time ago—I made up my mind. After Collin, I will never let another person abuse me, my love, or my life."

Tristen opened his mouth, then closed it. He clenched his jaw, searching for words, and finally said, "You want something I can't give you, Chelsea. You want love, commitment, a future— and I can barely get out of bed some days. I'm drowning in my own mess, and dragging you down with me is the one thing I won't do. Just go. Don't make this harder. Just . . . go."

The words hit her like a slap.

Chelsea looked back at him, shattered. Her eyes widened, her breath caught in her chest. For a moment, everything around her blurred—the beige walls, the sound of cars passing outside, the scent of his cologne.

She was right back in her past—watching her marriage crumble piece by piece, watching her younger self crying and trying to pull it all back together, begging God to make sense of how she ended up here. Tears rolled down her cheeks as she struggled to understand how, after everything she had done to support him, he could toss her love aside as if it didn't matter. As if she wasn't there for him. As if they hadn't built dreams together.

She felt undone. How could this be happening . . . again?

But not this time.

She felt undone yet stood her ground.

Chelsea turned and walked out of the apartment. The cold air hit her like a slap.

Tristen stood at the door, frozen. He watched her walk down the hallway—her white coat swaying with every step, her shoulders squared in heartbreak. His throat burned to call after her, but no words would come out. He wanted to go after her, to pull her into his arms one last time, but his legs wouldn't move.

He leaned against the doorframe and whispered, "I'm sorry."

Chelsea descended the stairs in a daze, her hand trembling as she called David.

"Can you come back and get me?" she asked, her voice barely above a whisper.

"I come," he said softly.

When David arrived, he looked at her tear-streaked face and said, "Lo siento, miss. I'm sorry. I tell you not to go. You're a good woman."

She didn't answer. She couldn't.

She sat in silence as the cab pulled away. Her reflection in the window looked like someone she no longer recognized. She called the airline and booked the next flight home.

Two years of dreams.

Two years of prayers.

Two years of carrying someone else's pain—gone in just a few minutes.

The flight home was a blur. Strangers offered concerned glances, but all she could say was, "I'm fine."

She had mastered the art of being fine.

She was fine when she was falling apart.
Fine when her heart was crushed.
Fine when the weight was too heavy to carry.
"I'm fine," she whispered again.
But deep down, she knew—
She wasn't fine.
Not even close.

Chapter Eight

The Woman in the Mirror

Chelsea walked out of the bathroom and sat on the bench at the foot of her bed. The room was still, but her mind was far from quiet.

How could something that began so beautifully end so painfully? she wondered.

Yes, they had their ups and downs, breakup after breakup, but they always seemed to find their way back to each other. Being apart had always felt harder. Tristen had shown her how to love again, and she had opened her heart and soul to him.

God, I fasted and prayed so many times to make sure this man was the one, she thought. I just wanted to get it right this time.

Since Collin, Tristen was the only man she had truly allowed in. From the day they met, it felt as though their spirits had intertwined. Even now, after all the heartbreak, she couldn't seem to let go.

Why can't I let go of you? she asked silently.

She closed her eyes and rubbed her face, searching for answers. Maybe it was because Tristen had always been a perfect gentleman—attentive, tender, and thoughtful. He showered her with sweet surprises and listened with a devotion that made her feel adored. His calm confidence was the opposite of Collin's controlling insecurity. With Tristen, she had started to believe the past was behind her.

You were everything Collin was not. But maybe that was the problem too, she reflected. Maybe I should've trusted God to heal those wounds instead of leaning on you.

She drew in a breath. In the end, you both broke me—one shattered my spirit, the other my heart.

Her thoughts were interrupted by the sharp ring of the

telephone. With a sigh, Chelsea walked over to her bedside and picked up the receiver.

"Hello?"

"Hi, Chelsea. It's Loretta."

"How are you?"

"I'm fine, but I actually called to check on you. You were heavy on my spirit this morning."

"Well, did you pray for me?"

"I always pray for you, but today, the Holy Spirit placed you so strongly on my heart that I couldn't ignore it."

Chelsea let out a soft laugh. "Why does God always tell on me? I feel like every time something is wrong, He tells you. I can't hide anything anymore."

Loretta chuckled. "Praise God for that gift. Is it Tristen again?"

"Bingo. I'm so tired of not being able to get him out of my head. Tired of wondering why it didn't work out."

"Chelsea, I believe it's time to let him go. You know I care for him deeply, but I also believe your season with him is over. God gives us all choices, and Tristen made some that led you both here. If only he had fully trusted God, maybe things would've been different."

"I agree with you in my head, Loretta. But my heart still can't catch up."

"You've got to trust God with this one and tell your heart to follow. Otherwise, you might miss what God is trying to give you."

Chelsea exhaled. "I keep replaying everything—our last conversation, his tears, his apology. Loretta, he was getting better. The hardest parts were over. In a way, it felt like he used me to get over the hump, and when he was there, he was done with me. In that conversation, he said he wanted me to know he loved me, that it was hard being the man I needed when he felt like half a man himself . . . then all the promises about getting his life together . . ."

"What did you say to that?"

"I started crying. For the first time, he heard me cry. Usually, I was the strong one. He begged me to stop. He said I was killing him. I told him he'd already killed me. And I hung up."

"Chelsea, that's intense."

"I wasn't being dramatic, Loretta—I was being real. It felt like death. You told me he was about to propose. I went from planning a wedding to a breakup in less than twenty-four hours. After investing so much of myself, I walked away with nothing but a broken heart."

"That's a lot to carry."

"And now I sit here, rethinking everything—how we started, the secrecy because of work, how I made more money than him, how he and Daniel never connected. But then I remember how he was all the things Collin wasn't—charming, spiritual, romantic . . ."

"Chelsea."

"Thoughtful, poetic . . ."

"CHELSEA."

"What?"

"Stop. Do you hear yourself? You're re-romanticizing him. You can't keep doing that. Focusing on how he was different from Collin doesn't make him right for you. You need more than someone who simply isn't your past."

"I wasn't doing that."

"Oh, really?"

"Okay, maybe a little."

"Here's the truth—Tristen lacked the most important thing: the ability to trust God and lean on His Word. Until he did that, the two of you would always be unequally yoked. He had demons he needed to confront. You can't enter into a marriage full of unresolved issues. It will only catch up to you. Marriage is the only equation where one plus one equals one. That means one whole person, plus another whole person, equals one whole couple. You can't be half a person looking for someone to complete you. It will never work."

"I know all about being unequally yoked, Loretta—2 Corinthians 6:14. I've preached on it. It's about believers not being yoked with unbelievers. Tristen believed."

"Maybe. But faith is lived, not just claimed. His refusal to trust God fully affected everything—and dragged you down, too. He was running from so many things. You've got a powerful purpose, Chelsea. God wasn't going to let someone derail that."

"I prayed so hard for him. I stayed up nights when he called in pain. I gave him all I had. Was it all for nothing?"

"No. Maybe your purpose in his life was to carry him through that season. To intercede for him. If you hadn't, who knows where he'd be now?"

Chelsea trembled. Tears spilled down her cheeks.

"I just want to be happy, Loretta. I want to come home to someone who wraps me in love. I've carried everyone for so long. When is it my turn?"

"It will come—in God's timing."

"I used to think Collin's strong arms would make me feel safe. Funny how the thing that drew me in was what I eventually ran from."

"Then remember what you once told me: we must run to God to rebuild where others have torn us down. Only He can fill the deepest wounds. No man can do that."

With a small laugh, Chelsea replied, "Why didn't you just tell me to hush back then?"

"Because when God speaks through you, I listen. Now I'm returning your words."

"Gee, thanks."

"I remember how broken you were after Tristen. Your pain was so deep I could feel it in my own heart."

"It was paralyzing. I sat right here—numb. Screaming, pounding the floor, and still the pain wouldn't go away. Two years wasted . . . for what?"

"I remember. You called me and sobbed the words 'It hurts.' I cried with you because I felt it too. And that's how God is— our pain becomes His."

"I kept thanking Him, even in the pain. I knew He was either protecting or preparing me. I just didn't understand it. But now I try to remember Job. He never got the answers to all his questions, but he still trusted that God reigned. And even when I struggle, I try to do the same."

"That's it, Chelsea. God still reigns. Hold on to that truth. Let it carry you forward."

Chelsea sighed. "I just wish I could stop crying about this. It makes me feel weak."

Loretta took a slow breath. "Chelsea, sweetheart, crying doesn't make you weak. It makes you human. Sometimes, the only way we can release some things is through silent tears or really ugly cries. But that water heals something in us. Do you hear me? Cry, release, and move forward, baby girl."

"Thanks, Loretta."

"No, thank you. We had church today. Read Psalm 23 later."

"Okay. Who's praying out—me or you?"

"I've got it. Father God, help Chelsea release the past and hold fast to You. Remind her that You didn't bring her this far to leave her. Strengthen her heart and direct her steps. Let her walk in peace, clarity, and joy. In Jesus' name, amen."

Chelsea smiled. "Thank you, Loretta."

"Remember, Jesus reigns."

Chelsea stood, a quiet strength settling over her. This is my last trip down memory lane, she promised. It's time for closure.

She decided to revisit her old journal and letters from Tristen one final time—and then burn them. As she rummaged through her drawer, her hand landed on a red velvet journal. A few cards from Tristen slipped out.

She paused, remembering how he'd sent her seven cards before his cruise—one for each day he'd be gone, each envelope numbered. She'd treasured that sweet gesture, and the memory made her smile.

She recalled how he'd returned claiming a divine encounter— how God had revealed the pain he'd caused her. He said he'd seen the weight of his words, the silence of her tears, the damage he'd refused to see. He apologized, said he never realized how deeply he'd hurt her, and swore he'd never do it again.

Yet . . . a month later, he left or pushed her away.

Chelsea sat on her bench, holding the journal, her resolve deepening. It was time to remember, release, and rise.

She opened the cover.

And began.

Chapter Nine

Ashes to Answers

The journal rested in Chelsea's lap like a sacred artifact—fragile, blood-red, velvet-bound. As she traced the edge of its spine with her fingers, she hesitated.

Was she really ready to go back?

She had told Loretta she would burn it: the journal, the letters, the memories—everything. But even now, a whisper inside begged her to read. Just once more. One last look before letting go.

She opened the cover, and time unraveled.

Inside were scribbled prayers, tear-streaked confessions, entries she had written on nights when her heart couldn't bear the weight alone. Her words bled with longing, frustration, denial, love, and sorrow.

She turned a page, and a folded card fluttered to the floor.

It was one of the cruise letters—Tristen's writing still crisp, still familiar. She had forgotten how thoughtful he had been on that trip. Seven letters, one for each day he would be away, sealed and numbered like tiny treasures. His way of making sure she felt seen, even in his absence.

Chelsea picked it up and read silently:

> *Day three: I miss the sound of your voice. I imagine you reading this while curled up in bed, your hair pulled back, and that tiny crease between your brows when you're focused. You always say I notice everything. I do. I see you, Chelsea. I see all of you.*

A lump formed in her throat.

She'd tried to forget that conversation, but the memory had a way of finding her.

She remembered the phone call that followed his return—

the tremor in his voice, the strain between guilt and hope. He said he'd had a divine experience on that ship, that God had shown him visions: her crying alone in her car, lying in bed clutching her phone, trying not to dial his number. He said the pain hit him like a wave, that it broke him open.

"I had no idea how deeply I hurt you," he had whispered. "But I saw it. I saw it all."

She had believed him. Believed the tears in his voice, the conviction in his silence. She had hoped.

Chelsea closed the card, her fingers trembling slightly. The warmth of the memory had turned cold. She knew now what she hadn't wanted to admit then—remorse doesn't always mean change. And love doesn't always mean it's meant to last.

She turned back to the journal and began to read:

JANUARY 12

I don't recognize myself anymore. I look in the mirror and see someone who is waiting to be chosen. Waiting to be enough. But I already am. God, remind me that I already am.

JANUARY 20

His voice cracks when he says he loves me. Mine doesn't. Mine screams it in silence. Why does love always seem to echo louder when it's leaving?

FEBRUARY 1

Lord, I prayed for him. I covered him. I believed for him. I gave pieces of myself I didn't know I had left.

If love is patient and kind, why does mine feel like war?

FEBRUARY 15

Today I felt peace for five whole minutes. That's progress, right?

Chelsea exhaled and closed the journal. She didn't want to read anymore. She didn't need to read anymore. The turmoil wasn't good for her. She held it to her chest for a moment, then stood and walked to her fireplace. She set the journal down beside her and reached for the lighter.

But first, she knelt.

"God," she whispered, "thank You for letting me love. Even when it hurt. Even when it broke me. Because it also helped me grow. I release him now. I release what was, what could've been, and what I kept wishing for. I choose wholeness. I choose You."

She lit the first corner of the journal and watched the flames slowly consume the velvet binding. The paper curled, turned black, then to ash. Smoke rose gently toward the ceiling, like a prayer finally released.

When the last ember faded, Chelsea stood quietly in the glow of the firelight. Something inside her had shifted—not erased but freed.

No more pretending she didn't still hurt. No more waiting for closure to come from anyone but God.

This was it.

The end of mourning.

And the beginning of a new chapter she would write for herself.

Chapter Ten

A Sacred Rise

Chelsea trembled on her knees. She couldn't believe this day had finally arrived.

God, how could this be happening? How could You take someone like me—flawed, unworthy—and call me to be one of your chosen vessels?

The awe of the moment anchored her in place. She remained frozen, overwhelmed. Her family sat behind her in the pews, their pride nearly tangible. What a journey it had been for them all.

Lynda squeezed Peter's hand, her eyes fixed on their daughter at the altar.

"Peter, can you believe this is happening?"

Peter leaned closer, whispering in her ear, "And to think, you thought she joined a cult when she left the Catholic Church for the Protestant Church."

Lynda nudged him with her elbow and shot him a glare. "You were worried too!"

"Sure, but I didn't go around wailing, 'Woe is me, my baby's forsaken her faith! She's with some Protestant preacher draining her bank account!'"

Lynda pinched his arm. "Stop it. This is sacred."

Peter grinned, kissed her cheek, and quieted.

As she relaxed, Lynda's eyes returned to Chelsea. *What is she thinking right now?* she wondered.

Chelsea closed her eyes, breathing deeply to capture the gravity of the moment. What a journey.

She recalled the arguments she and her mother had when she left Catholicism. The debates over theology, the deep rifts that formed. Despite trying to explain why she needed more spiritual nourishment, her mother saw only rebellion.

God, You turned a mess into a miracle. Thank You for

softening her heart.

The bishop's voice echoed through the sanctuary.

"Do you trust that you are inwardly moved by the Holy Ghost to take upon you the Office of the Ministry in the Methodist Church, to serve God for the promotion of His glory and the edifying of His people?"

In the congregation, Collin sat with Matthew in his lap, watching the mother of his child with bittersweet admiration.

She looks so beautiful. I wish I could tell her. I wish we were going home together tonight.

He shifted in his seat, trying to focus on the ceremony.

"Do you unfeignedly believe all the canonical Scriptures of the Old and New Testament?"

Lynda sat taller, lifting her chin. You did it, baby.

Despite her reservations, Lynda had come to see a strength in Chelsea she never expected. She seemed lighter, wiser, more grounded. And somehow, Lynda felt a part of that transformation.

You've fulfilled a calling I once considered for myself, Lynda thought.

Earlier that morning, Lynda had finally shared her secret—a vow nearly taken, a life almost abandoned.

"I never told many people this," she had begun. "But I once tried to take a vow of silence. I was ready to become a nun."

Chelsea had stared in disbelief. "You're serious?"

"I was heartbroken. Your father broke up with me when we were young. My family disapproved of him, and he couldn't take the pressure. I was devastated. When I saw him later with another woman—a family friend, no less—I thought my life was over."

"What happened?"

"I ran to the church, to Father Martin, and begged to be admitted to the convent. I was ready to give it all up. But he refused. He told me I was running away, not answering a call."

"Wow."

"Then I told my mother. She broke down and begged me not to go silent. She said losing my voice would kill her. She didn't know I already felt dead inside."

"And then?"

"Then, God stepped in. Your father found me sobbing on a curb. He said nothing—just held me with his eyes. We knew in that moment we were meant to be. A week later, we were married in a simple ceremony. No fanfare. Just us, two witnesses, a judge—and God."

Lynda's voice cracked. "And that's why today means so much to me. I almost became a silent nun. But you, my daughter, are being ordained as a minister. What I couldn't become, you have surpassed."

Chelsea had wrapped her arms around her mother, tears streaming. "I had no idea."

Now, kneeling at the altar, those words returned. Her mother's pride was a balm to old wounds. Chelsea could feel her gaze, hear her unspoken cheer: I'm here, baby. I'm proud of you.

The bishop's final prayer thundered through the sanctuary. Oil was poured over Chelsea's head. Her shoulders shook with silent sobs—not of sadness but of surrender.

In the pew, Lynda wept too. The circle had closed. A vow unfulfilled by one generation had become a divine assignment in the next.

And in that sacred space, surrounded by prayer, legacy, and love, Chelsea rose—not just as a minister but as a woman wholly called, fully chosen, and beautifully redeemed.

Chapter Eleven

Seven Years Between Us

Chelsea forced herself to steady her breathing and focus. The sanctuary around her hummed with quiet movement—soft voices, measured footsteps, the gentle rustle of fabric—but her mind was still catching up to what God had just done. Everything felt surreal, suspended between what had been and what was about to begin.

Oh, God, she prayed silently. I remember when I first began to believe You were calling me to be a minister. I couldn't fathom it. Why me—the ex-Catholic, the divorcée, the girl with a world of issues? Me? Why me? And now I'm here. Me.

It felt as though the last seven years were unfolding before her eyes in a single breath: the nights she'd pleaded with God for confirmation of His call, the long hours at Bible college feeding her hunger to understand His Word, and the dreams—vivid, relentless dreams—of herself preaching and teaching, visions she'd once tried so hard to silence. Now they danced through her mind all at once, shimmering like fragments of prophecy finally fulfilled.

I still wouldn't believe You after all that, would I? she whispered inwardly. I kept testing You, asking for signs I thought were impossible. But even those things were possible with You, Father. I'm amazed You didn't give up on me or strike me down for my stubborn heart. I just couldn't see it. I couldn't believe it. Why me?

Chelsea drew a slow, steady breath as another memory stirred—the final dream that left no room for doubt. She hadn't understood it all, but she knew God was telling her to go and preach His Word. What made that dream unforgettable was who appeared in it: her mother—the person she feared would never accept her calling—and her assistant pastor, a woman who had quietly mothered her through the pain of divorce.

Chelsea closed her eyes and let the dream return.

She found herself standing in a small Catholic church, quiet and drenched in soft light. Ribbons of color streamed through stained glass, painting the pews in shifting hues. The air was heavy with incense and something sacred she couldn't name.

At the back sat her assistant pastor, Reverend Jacqueline, eyes fixed on her with a stare so piercing it stopped Chelsea in her tracks. It wasn't condemnation; it was knowing, as though she were trying to speak through her eyes alone.

Does she know? Chelsea wondered. Does she know God called me to preach? Or does she think I'm unworthy? What has God shown her?

Before she could move toward her, the scene shifted. The church dissolved, and she was suddenly standing in her parents' bedroom.

Her mother and father spoke as if she'd been there all night. Their words cut deep—questions about her faith, her decision to leave the Catholic Church, disappointment disguised as concern. Chelsea pleaded, voice trembling, "I'm only doing what God asked me to do."

But her mother turned away, tired. "I can't take any more of this," she said.

A rush of air, and Chelsea was back in the same Catholic church. The same light. The same ache. Her heart burned from the constant need to defend her calling. She scanned the sanctuary for Reverend Jacqueline but saw only her parents seated near the front.

Then came that voice—deep, steady, familiar. Her pastor was preaching from the altar.

Panic rose. What if Mom causes a scene? Chelsea couldn't bear another confrontation—not here. She slipped past them and sat alone, lowering her head. Tears spilled as she whispered, God, why does obedience hurt so much?

A hand rested on her shoulder.

She turned—it was Reverend Jacqueline. The assistant pastor reached for her hand, guiding her gently beside her. Then she pulled Chelsea close, pressing her head against her chest. Chelsea wept—the release fierce and holy, as if all her pain had finally found its resting place.

When her tears subsided, Reverend Jacqueline lifted her chin and met her eyes—silent but certain—as if to say, You're strong enough now.

At the altar, the sermon ended. A nun stepped forward, her voice echoing through the church. "Someone here is called to preach."

Reverend Jacqueline took the microphone, a knowing smile playing on her lips. "She's not lying." Her gaze found Chelsea's. "What she speaks—you already know."

No one else seemed to hear. The words hung in the air, suspended between heaven and her heart.

When the mass ended, Chelsea whispered, "I have to talk to you."

Reverend Jacqueline's smile softened. "Make an appointment."

And in that moment, Chelsea knew: God had already gone before her. The dream wasn't random—it was confirmation. The fear remained, but its power was gone. She had heard heaven speak.

* * *

A few weeks later, when Chelsea finally mustered enough courage to tell her assistant pastor that she felt she was called to preach the Word. She walked up to her with fear and trembling and asked if she could set up an appointment to speak. Surprisingly, her pastor never asked why she wanted to talk, instead instructing her to come to her office after service on Sunday. And so, the wheels were set in motion.

Chelsea didn't know if she should be happy or sad. She didn't even know what she would say to her assistant pastor. As a result, she spent the next few days rehearsing her speech in an effort not to make a fool of herself.

When the day came, she was terrified. She wasn't sure what her assistant pastor would see when she looked at Chelsea. Would she see the same woman who had walked into her office years ago, pregnant and in the midst of a divorce? Would she see someone who was stronger now or someone who was weak and frail? Would she see someone who was called by God, or would she see a woman who was scared and confused?

After service on Sunday, Chelsea went up to Reverend Jacqueline's office. She knocked on the door and meekly said, "Excuse me, Reverend Jacquie."

Reverend Jacqueline stepped away from her desk and walked toward the door. "Yes. What can I do for you?"

Chelsea could feel the knots in her stomach tightening. Didn't she remember they had an appointment?

"Well, I'm Chelsea Stevens, and I asked you a little over a week ago if we could speak. You told me to come to your office after service today."

"Oh, yes, I forgot. What did you want to talk to me about?"

Chelsea looked around the hallway to see if anyone could hear her. Then in a timid, trembling voice, she said, "Well, I wanted to talk to you about . . . ummm . . . I . . . I think . . . God has called me to preach."

By the time she got that statement out, her whole body was shaking, and she was mortified at her childlike rambling.

Reverend Jacqueline moved a little closer. "Well, there is someone using my office right now. Let's see if we can speak in my husband's office."

Oh, great, Chelsea thought as they walked into his office. As if telling her assistant pastor were not bad enough, now she might have to tell her pastor, too. He was even scarier than Reverend Jacqueline.

When they walked into his office, he was sitting at his desk. Her assistant pastor sat down at the other end of the room and asked Chelsea to join her.

Now she had to say this in earshot of him, too? She wasn't prepared for all of this. It was too much for her. It was bad enough that she had to say it out loud in front of one of them, but now both of them? She was ready to die.

At this point, she couldn't even remember the speech she had rehearsed. What was she going to say? How could she communicate that she felt God was calling her to be a preacher? Chelsea began to shake. She was so embarrassed because she couldn't stop shaking, and she knew it was quite visible to her assistant pastor. If only her body would stop betraying her. If only her hands would be still. If only the words would come out of her mouth.

Her assistant pastor calmly asked, "So, talk to me, Chelsea?"

Chelsea looked up at her and tried to remember what she was going to say, but her mind was blank. Instead, a jumble of muffled words came out.

Oh, great, how is she going to believe that I am called to preach if I can't even speak? God, please help me find the right words to say. Please, Father. You know how hard this is.

Chelsea whispered with a trembling voice, "Um, I believe that God has called me into the ministry." She just blurted it out and hoped that it sounded somewhat coherent.

Her assistant pastor chuckled and called over to her husband, saying, "Look at Chelsea, she is here to announce her calling, and she is just shaking like a leaf." Pastor Briceson looked up for a moment and said, "Is that so?" then continued to do his work.

Chelsea was beyond mortified and embarrassed.

"Chelsea, this is a serious matter and something that we need more time to discuss. Why don't you call my assistant tomorrow and set up an appointment so we can sift through this further?"

"Okay," she agreed, and a few minutes later, she was gone. What a relief that was to her. At least the hard part is over, she thought.

After another meeting, her assistant pastor placed her in a ministerial training class and told her that she would have to go to seminary. A year and a half later, Chelsea was called to preach her first sermon in front of the church body. Three years later, she now found herself kneeling before the bishop to be ordained.

What a journey it had been—school at night, ministerial classes on the weekends, church board examinations, annual questioning before the bishop, new ministerial responsibilities, and now finally, ordination.

"Lord, I thought this day would never come."

The bishop now stood over Chelsea. He placed his hands over her head as she kissed a Bible. He prayed over her.

He then said, "You have gone down as Sister Chelsea Stevens, and when you rise, you will be the Reverend Chelsea Stevens, in the name of the Father, Son, and Holy Ghost."

And that was it. She was now Reverend Stevens to the church body.

As the sun set on one part of her life, it rose on another. At thirty years of age, her ministry had, in a way, just begun.

Tears rolled down her face.

"Thank You, Father, for allowing this day to finally come. I know that this represents the beginning of many lonely days, hardships, joys, blessings, and challenges. But I also know that You will see me through. To whom much is given, much is required. Whatever You want from me is yours."

Chapter Twelve

The Truth About Starting Over

Chelsea glanced at the clock. 1:30 a.m. "I can't do this for another night," she said to herself.

This was day three. For three nights in a row, she had tossed and turned. She hated this. She couldn't handle any type of conflict in her life, and now here she was, in the thick of it. For what?

Finally, she had met someone she liked, and now, seven weeks into their relationship, they were fighting. Langston hadn't contacted her in four days, which was truly a new thing. He went from ten messages a day to nothing literally overnight. Was he ghosting her?

"Why is this happening to me?" she shouted to herself. She sat up in bed and began to cry.

"God, I can't do this again. I just can't."

She was careful not to wake her visiting parents. Chelsea knew if they heard her, they would be worried, and she couldn't have that.

"God, why is this affecting me like this? This is crazy. How can a man I've only known for seven weeks have this kind of hold on me? Oh, I can't take it."

She got out of bed and began to pace and pray, pray and pace. After about forty-five minutes of that, she thought it might help to fall to her knees and pray. She prayed for peace, she prayed for patience, she prayed for Langston to stop playing these stupid games, but most of all, she prayed for sleep.

"I can't do this anymore. My kids aren't even with me this week, and I've spent the entire week suffering over what? An email? A text? No phone call? God, what's going on with me?"

She looked at the clock. It now said 3:00 a.m.

God, help me.

"Okay, I'll read my Bible."

So she read and read and read. She read a few chapters from Numbers, Samuel, and Matthew.

Four a.m.

Chelsea closed the Bible, turned out the light, and said, "I'm going to bed."

Four-thirty a.m.

She was still tossing and turning.

She couldn't understand what was going on. It had begun so wonderfully. He had his eyes on her for a while. He said that he had noticed her for the first time at a church celebration. He claimed that he was smitten with her and immediately asked a close friend, a visiting pastor who was also invited to the celebration, if he knew who she was. In a fortuitous turn of events, the pastor not only knew Chelsea well but also told Langston that she really looked up to him as one of her fathers in ministry.

Months went by, and he waited for an opportunity to speak to her. It finally came when he was asked to preach at her church. She was on her way out, and he was coming in. When Chelsea looked over at him standing in the corner, he looked somewhat nervous. A fellow minister introduced them, and they began a light conversation.

She joked with him for a brief moment and told him that she was on her way out but would stay so that she could pray him through.

He said, "It's okay. You have your coat on. You can go about your business."

She insisted that she would stay and proceeded to put her clergy robe back on. They joked for a few minutes, and she went into the sanctuary and began to pray.

After the service, they ran into each other again. She asked him if he felt her praying him through, and he said, "Yes, and I very much appreciated it." They conversed for a few more minutes until someone interrupted to speak with him. Chelsea walked away and headed home.

That was the last time she saw or spoke to him for months. Then one day, out of the blue, she was standing outside a hotel where she was scheduled to attend a conference. As fate would have it, Langston and his pastor friend happened to be passing through the conference. When the pastor saw Chelsea, he walked right over and asked if she had met Langston.

Chelsea, oblivious to what was going on and running late, said, "I think I've met him before." When Langston approached her, she gave him a business handshake and said it was nice to see him again. She then turned around and continued her conversation with their pastor friend. A few minutes later, the two of them walked away. Until next time. And there was indeed a next time, which ignited the relationship that was now breaking her.

Langston later told her that he was very disappointed that day. At first, he said that he thought she was cold and cruel because she ignored the twinkle in his eyes as he hoped to get to know her better. He gave her a hard time about that day for a while, but during one of their first three-hour marathon conversations, he admitted that he had high hopes of getting to know her that day—only for her to crush them. His exact words were etched in Chelsea's mind because they touched her.

She closed her eyes and imagined him saying it to her all over again in his deep, sultry voice.

"Chelsea, our encounter at the conference was an issue because I wanted to speak to you. Speak to you at length. It wasn't just about me . . . or maybe it was . . . maybe it was about us. I wanted to get to know you. I was very smitten with you when I first met you. I immediately asked about you. I remembered you and wanted to see you again." The words felt perfect. They felt thoughtful and hopeful. They felt intelligent and intriguing. And that was Langston to her.

Just remembering his words made her angry. He would always say things like that to her. That's what made the fallout that much harder. He had an ability to titillate her with his words but yet always disappointed her with his actions.

"Ahhhhh!" she screamed. "Why did you come into my life? What kind of cruel game is this? You pursued me. Why? Just to see if you could get me?"

Memories of their first few weeks together flooded her mind.

In a short period of time, while she was on vacation, they spent countless hours talking via email, text, and phone. She remembered how he would tell her things like, "Oh, Chelsea, I'm reading your texts in between sets of twenty-five pushups and am met by beauty."

What crap, she thought.

He would send his photo via text and ask her to do the same because he wanted to see her in her "sunshine glory."

More crap.

It was so odd to Chelsea how this man could get her attention in such a major way. He was very different from the other men she dated, which might have been part of his appeal. He was not the debonair stud that would make her do a double take. He wasn't overly funny, encouraging, or complimentary, and certainly didn't sing to her like Tristen.

He didn't make her feel safe with his brute strength like Collin. He had none of that. As a matter of fact, his jokes were a bit corny, he had a subtle arrogance about him that annoyed her, and he wasn't overly inviting in his approach. His looks were average at best—except for his six-foot-five frame, which Chelsea loved. Still, he had a certain charm and take-charge attitude that swayed her.

In a world where it appeared chivalry was dead, a man who opened doors and walked on the outside to protect his dame was very appealing. Not to mention he was well-traveled, and it showed when he spoke. Langston would challenge Chelsea mentally, and that excited her.

Name it, he said it. He caught Chelsea completely off guard, and it caused her to begin to lower the drawbridge that protected her heart and separated her from all suitors.

"It was your words that did it," Chelsea said dryly to herself. "What happened to rule number one, girl? Never fall prey to a man's words. Let him prove himself by his deeds."

She cringed at the thought of allowing him to reel her in. This was the first time in her life she had ever let herself get caught up in a situation like this. She fell fast and was getting ghosted. Seriously?

He probably read one of those 'how to be a playa' books and tried all of those lines on me and half the women he came across.

At this point, all she could do was laugh at the situation. Not because it was funny, but because it felt better than crying. She was so frustrated about how she let his sweet words melt her.

It had been a while since she allowed a man to get into "that" space with her. He would send her random emails saying things like, "You're amazing." Or he would text her, stating how sweet she was or tell her how he was "compelled to be with her" as he enjoyed her company a great deal.

He told her that he wasn't playing any games, and she believed him. Did she believe it so easily because he was a minister? But the reality is they're human too. They're regular men and women, and they have faults too. How stupid was she for doing that? How could she have fallen for his trap and allowed herself to be seduced by his words and touch?

Why the hell did I believe him when he said I was the first woman in his adult life that he could see having children with, or that he was becoming susceptible to falling in love with me?

Why? Why? Why? Did I allow myself to fall for those lines? In a couple of months, at that?

Chelsea sighed to herself. She was at an absolute loss for words and in deep need of some sleep.

Does someone who doesn't have real feelings just text you every morning when they wake up or every night before they go to bed? Does someone who is just playing a game constantly tell you how much they miss you and wish they were there with you? Have I been out of the dating scene so long that I can't see the signs when someone is trying to play a game?

Chelsea sat on her bed, shaking her head, wondering how she had allowed herself to get sucked in.

BUT HE'S A MINISTER, GOD. Doesn't that count for anything? Shouldn't I have been able to trust him? How can he preach love while living in hypocrisy? I thought You sent him to me, God. I waited so long and so patiently. I thought You sent him.

She tried to figure out what signs she might have missed.

I just don't get it. When I tried to pull back a little, all he did was come at me stronger. I thought that was You, God, trying to confirm that he was the one. What did I miss?

Her mind was drawn to the foreboding feeling she had after their first week of intense conversation. She kept wondering if this was real. Deep down, she felt that he was going to hurt her, but she didn't want to give in to those feelings because he pursued her so intensely—down to their marathon three-hour conversations and countless texts each day.

Why didn't I trust my instincts? But you were so good at your game.

Chelsea curled up in a fetal position on her bed and began to rock back and forth.

Why can't I just get you out of my mind?

But her mind betrayed her as memories of his courtship flooded in like a raging river.

Chelsea moaned. She remembered how, when it was time for her to come home from vacation, he insisted on speaking to her that night, even though her flight was going to get in after midnight. He would not take no for an answer, even though she said it would be too late. His response was, "I'll keep you up with my humor."

He always had a response when he wanted something.

Chelsea balled her fists and placed them over her ears as she tried to make the memories go away. But they wouldn't stop.

She remembered how ironic it was that the two of them were on vacation at the same time. Being removed from all distractions only intensified the beginning of their relationship. He even wanted to fly directly to her town so they could go on their first date on his way home.

Although that didn't work out, they agreed to meet for

dinner the following day. She drove to him because he was stuck catching up on work. When she arrived at his apartment, they tried to decide what they were going to do—maybe go to the movies or out to dinner—but Chelsea was content just staying in and watching a movie over pizza. She didn't need the bells and whistles to be happy. She was content just being in his company.

He agreed, and they spent that evening enjoying each other. After the movie, they spent three hours just talking. They watched the sunset together from his apartment as he played soft music and lit some candles. He then told her about his childhood, read her poetry, and they simply enjoyed each other as time flew by.

Before they knew it, nearly five hours had passed. Nothing physical occurred; everything was more spiritual and emotional. When she realized it was after 10:00 p.m. and she had to teach a class for her church early the next morning, she said her goodbyes. Langston walked her to her car. She offered him her hand to shake as a joke, but he grabbed her and gave her a big hug. And that was it.

They agreed to see each other on Monday. She had a meeting for work near where he lived, and he said he would enjoy her company again. He rearranged his schedule to catch a later business flight and met her for lunch. They had a wonderful time. When they parted ways, he immediately texted her to tell her how much he once again enjoyed her company and would miss her. They talked about everything in that one short hour.

But then, like a wave of sudden guilt, he went into a full-fledged workaholic state, and things quickly changed. Their marathon conversations ended abruptly, and their communication was reduced to text messages.

Maybe this is when your true self came out. I mean, how long can anyone keep up an act?

All his texting annoyed her; after all, Chelsea hated texting as the primary form of communication in any relationship. It seemed to inhibit people from forming true connections. Even so, since this was so important to him and his favorite form of communication, she acquiesced. After a while, it didn't seem so bad. She began to enjoy seeing his name pop up on her phone throughout the day.

He would tell her about all his many trips, how tired he was, and that he was thinking about her. He would text her to say he just called out her name in his heart and mind. He said it all . . . over text.

See, Chelsea, that's what you get when you compromise your needs and relax your standards. Next thing you know, you find yourself out in left field, wondering how you got there with this person. Never again. But damn, Langston, you sure did play the role well. You seemed to be everything I always wanted in a man.

Their last date solidified that in Chelsea's mind . . . even how it unfolded.

She rolled over again in bed and took another deep breath.

Her mind drifted to one of the few live conversations they had over the last few weeks when Langston told her that he had just celebrated his thirty-seventh birthday. Chelsea asked him what he had done, and he said, "Nothing." She told him that she was going to put together a "birthday surprise" to celebrate with him. "After all, you only turn thirty-seven once," she teased. So they planned to get together the following weekend.

Chelsea spent the whole week trying to figure out how to help him relax and surprise him. She came up with a picnic theme and went to several stores, finally finding the perfect picnic basket, a matching blanket, his favorite bottle of wine, fruits, sandwiches, bottled water for her, soda, Godiva cookies, a DVD of a Broadway show he was itching to see, a book about the making of the play, and a mini-birthday cake for two. When she got to his apartment, he was blown away.

She remembered how they ate and tenderly talked for a while. He told her how the cake was perfect. It was the same color combination his mother always made for him as a child. He was in shock. He told her that he wished he could show her pictures of himself as a child with this very same cake. He then asked Chelsea if he could take her out and get her the chocolate cake he promised her during her last visit. He suggested they save cutting the cake she brought for the end of the evening. She happily agreed.

So they headed off to one of his favorite dessert spots, where they sat outside and shared dessert and great conversation. He told her about his childhood and some of his most precious moments. He spoke about the death of his father and the impact it had on him. He opened his heart to her as time passed. After spending a while at the restaurant, he asked her if she wanted to go for a walk. They walked and talked throughout his town, exploring some of his favorite shops as they strolled. At one point, he gently touched her arm, and butterflies fluttered throughout her body. When he asked her why she stepped back, she said that his touch was so gentle it gave her butterflies. He smiled and said, "Thank you."

After a while, he asked her if he could take her for a drive. She had spotted a house in the area that she had fallen in love with over eight years ago and told him about it. He asked if he could take her to see the house together. During the drive, he showed her around town and where he grew up. He shared stories from his youth and showed her the house where he was raised. He filled her head with sweet words and introduced her to his world, and she enjoyed every moment of it.

Finally, they found her dream house—the one she had decided years ago she would live in and raise her family. She wondered if he would be part of that dream. Would he be the man she spent the rest of her life with? It felt so perfect, and he seemed so right and so into her. He seemed like everything she had been waiting for.

For years, she had turned away all suitors because she felt nothing for them. Something was always missing. For years, she had guarded her heart because she could not bear to be hurt again like she had been with Tristen. She was so scared and would never let anyone in.

Tristen and Collin had taken almost all of her and left her for dead—one, she felt, had raped her physically; the other, emotionally. No more . . . she remembered thinking.

She couldn't be hurt anymore. She couldn't deal with any more nuts, anyone who tried to stalk her like Francis, or anyone who sent her secret flowers like Rubin, or anyone who approached her like all the Toms, Dicks, and Harrys she felt nothing for at all.

Chelsea yearned for love. She wanted true love that would sweep her off her feet and make her insides melt. Langston seemed to be doing it all. He would tell her how the things she said made him melt inside, which tickled her.

That night after the drive, they went back to his apartment to cut the cake. He blew out the candles and made a wish.

Chelsea asked him what he wished for, and he refused to tell her.

She said, "Don't you know the rule?"

He replied, "What rule?"

"You're supposed to tell the person closest to you what your wish is."

He jumped off the couch and ran away. As if that were her cue, she got up and chased him. He stopped short and wrapped his arms around her. He said that he greatly appreciated what she had done for him that night and would never forget it.

He pulled her close and tried to kiss her. Chelsea was caught off guard. She never let people get that close. It had been a long time since she had been in the arms of a man like this. It had now been two years since she had broken up with Tristen.

What was she to do? Even when she and Tristen were together, they rarely found themselves in that position because of his all-or-nothing rule. She had been starved for affection with him, and now, in a matter of weeks, Langston was going to fill that void.

At that moment, fear coursed through her body. What if she didn't remember how to kiss? She knew she had certainly had her share in the past, but it seemed like such a long time since those days. All of these thoughts flooded her mind as Langston tried to connect with her.

As his lips touched hers, she turned her face away. Wait, she thought. I want to kiss him.

She looked up at him and saw that his eyes were closed.

Hmm, she thought, he means business.

He continued to try. He gently kissed her face until their lips met. And when they did, he parted them with his.

She allowed him to enter her. It was so strange. It felt new to her. It was so intimate. It was so deep. He pulled her closer and held her tight. He began to rub her back, and Chelsea started to melt in his arms. She began to kiss his neck and ears. She squeezed closer to him as he continued to kiss her. This was too much for her at the moment, and she began to feel a little dizzy.

He whispered, "Your lips are so soft."

Without thinking, she blurted out, "It has been so long since I've allowed anyone to touch them. Years, actually." She could have kicked herself for saying that.

He whispered again, "I am honored," and began to caress her again. When they finally parted lips, she felt like her virtue had been poured out. It was so strange. She could barely stand and wondered if he noticed. Did he even know how she had let him in at that moment? He could never have known. Only she and God knew how she had let him into her secret place with just one kiss.

"Little did I know that was going to be my last time seeing you. Shoot, if I had known that, I might have kissed you some more."

She chuckled for a moment at that thought, then her stomach began to turn again.

"How could something that began so perfectly end so badly, God? Is this some type of cruel joke? All I wanted was a companion to share my heart and dreams."

The numbers on the clock seemed to fade as Chelsea's eyes began to feel heavy.

Chapter Thirteen

The Breaking Point

"Jennifer, can you please come in here now?"

Jennifer rolled her eyes and slowly rose from her desk. She pasted on a polite smile as she entered Langston's office.

"Yes, Langston? What can I do for you?"

"I wanted to apologize for being short with you earlier," he began, straightening the papers on his desk. "But I've told you several times—everything that leaves this office needs to be thoroughly proofread. These correspondences go to hundreds of people. They represent us. The last thing I need is for others to question the credibility of someone in my position."

Jennifer shifted on her feet, suddenly regretting her choice of heels. "I understand. And again, I'm sorry. It was just a small typo."

"No typo is small," Langston replied, his tone clipped. "Perception matters. I want people to see that rising professionals are just as capable—if not more so—than anyone else. We reflect our work."

Jennifer sighed internally. "I get it," she said. Then, without thinking, she added, "So, what's really bothering you?"

Langston's eyes narrowed. "What's that supposed to mean?"

She backpedaled. "Nothing. It just seems like you've been a little on edge lately."

"I'm fine."

"Okay. Well, I'm gonna go to lunch. Want me to bring anything back?"

"Do you mean 'going to'?" he corrected.

Jennifer clenched her jaw. "Silly me—speaking broken English in your presence."

Langston smirked. "Exactly. And no, thank you. I'm not hungry. Just shut the door on your way out."

"Sure thing, boss."

As she exited, she muttered under her breath, "He needs a good screw. Might loosen him up."

Langston loosened his tie and stared blankly at his screen. His inbox glowed with Chelsea's last message, which he had reread at least ten times:

Langston,

It's hard for me to understand how, after your request that we communicate more, you haven't returned any of my calls. You said if I needed to talk, I should reach out. I did. And nothing. One of my biggest values is follow-through—saying what you mean and meaning what you say. You didn't call Saturday like you promised. I understand you may have gotten caught up, but not even five minutes all weekend? Not even a quick acknowledgment? I'm starting to feel like an afterthought—and that's not something I'm used to. I wish it weren't this way, but the excitement I once felt is beginning to fade.

~Chelsea

Langston clenched his fists.

How could she say she was losing interest? After everything?

His mind drifted to their first kiss. She had melted in his arms, her body trembling, her lips soft and inviting. She was reserved, yet something wild lingered beneath the surface. She fascinated him.

He closed his eyes and began to fantasize, recalling every detail of her touch, her scent. His hand slipped below his desk . . . until the phone rang.

"Hello," he snapped, irritated.

"Yo, man, what's up? I've been trying to reach you all week."

Langston exhaled. "What's up, Eric?"

"That's how you greet your big brother?"

"I was in the middle of something."

"You always are. You work too damn much."

"I'm just a man trying to make it in this world."

"Oh, spare me the martyr speech, Rerun."

Langston's patience wore thin. "You know I hate that."

Eric chuckled. "Relax. What's got you so uptight?"

Langston was silent.

"Still getting dissed by women like back in the day? 'No Wrap'?"

"You and Angelo always made fun of me—my stutter, my voice, my ideas. I'm sick of it."

"C'mon, Langston. You're the golden child. Pa always had your back."

"Yeah, because you two never let me breathe. I always felt alone."

"Maybe we stuck together 'cause you were always trying to prove you were better than us."

"I never tried to make you look bad. You did that just fine on your own."

Eric sighed. "Where's this coming from?"

"Nowhere. What do you want?"

"Auntie Janice is home this weekend. Angelo can't make it. Can you fly in and keep her company?"

"You're already there. Why can't you?"

"I've got plans. Besides, you're her favorite."

"I'll see what I can do."

"Peace, Preacherman."

Langston hung up hard. His thoughts drifted again—back to Chelsea, back to her message.

Why is she pressing me so hard? Doesn't she know who I am? He had responsibilities—speeches, meetings, a schedule most couldn't handle.

Still, he couldn't stop thinking about her.

He picked up his iPhone and reread her text: When you get back to your office, can you have your assistant schedule a call? I can't seem to get even two minutes with you.

Langston felt heat rising in his chest.

I told her from the beginning—I don't do conflict. Why is that so hard for her to understand?

Yes, she was intelligent. Beautiful. Intriguing. But lately, she reminded him too much of Selena. Another driven, career-first woman who had crushed his heart.

His mother had warned him.

"Baby," she'd said, "you need a woman who wants to be a helpmeet, not a powerhouse."

He could still hear her voice.

Maybe Ma was right, he thought. It always ends the same.

Still, something about Chelsea was different. Wasn't it?

Langston groaned and rubbed his temples. I'm not ready to respond.

He shut down his computer, grabbed his coat, and left the office.

"God," he whispered as he stepped into the hallway. "What am I supposed to do with a woman like Chelsea?"

Chapter Fourteen

When the Masks Fall Off

Chelsea scanned the bustling restaurant, hoping not to see a single familiar face. She didn't have the strength to fake a smile. Once seated, she tucked herself into the corner of the booth, as if the shadows might shield her from the weight of the week.

A tall, perky blonde appeared beside the table. "Hi! I'm Sandy. Can I start you off with a drink?"

Chelsea wanted to say, Yes—vodka, double, make it quick. But those days were behind her. At least, that's what she kept telling herself.

"Strawberry lemonade, please."

"Would you like an appetizer?"

"Not yet. I'm waiting for someone."

"Sounds good. I'll be back in a jiffy."

Chelsea offered a forced smile. The moment Sandy left, she glanced at her watch. Nicky was late—but not surprisingly so.

Just as she reached for her phone, the clack of heels echoed through the restaurant. Chelsea looked up and immediately recognized the diva strut. Nicky glided in, fierce and unapologetic. She was decked out in a crisp white pantsuit, her bob freshly styled, and candy-apple red stilettos clicking as if she owned the place.

"Hey, girl."

Chelsea shrank further into the booth. "Why are you so dressed up? You're making me look like a bum."

"Because I have standards," Nicky said, sliding into the seat. "And right now, you look like you've been crying for three days straight."

"Try three nights. No sleep." Chelsea peeled off her sunglasses, revealing the damage.

"Oh, Lord." Nicky laughed. "My eyes! You could've warned

me."

Chelsea tried not to smile. "Glad my pain is entertaining."

"Girl, don't be dramatic. You're giving casual chic vibes . . . emphasis on casual."

The waitress returned with her lemonade. "Will it just be the two of you today?"

"Yes," Chelsea replied.

"Great. I'll give you a few minutes to look at the menu."

As soon as Sandy left, Nicky turned back to her. "Alright. What's really going on?" Chelsea hesitated. "Langston." Nicky froze. "I thought things were good between you two. You had that stupid dreamy look on your face just last week."

Chelsea shrugged. "It's like he disappeared. No explanation. No nothing."

Nicky leaned in, serious now. "Start from the beginning."

Chelsea took a deep breath and began.

"Last Saturday, I was in a weird headspace. I'd spent all day on the phone helping people through their mess, and it drained me. I was already annoyed because Langston barely responded to my text the night before—said he was 'busy,' like always. So when he called, I was cold. Not mean, just . . . distant. I figured he'd notice and ask what was wrong."

"Let me guess—he didn't."

"Nope. Just acted normal. So when he asked what I was doing, I told him I started watching a movie we planned to see together. I was hoping it'd trigger something—some kind of emotion. But he just said, 'That's okay. I'll watch it again by myself.' Like it was no big deal."

Nicky rolled her eyes. "Wow. You think playing games is ever a good idea?"

"I felt guilty after we hung up. So I called back, apologized, and tried to explain I'd had a rough day. He was nice about it, actually. Said he could tell something was off, but figured it was just one of those days."

"Still no excuse."

"I know. But we had a decent conversation, and when I asked if we could see each other the next day, he said, 'Absolutely.' Then he mentioned he had to go to church, visit his aunt, and work out—that was it. No real plan, just kind of a vague maybe."

"Chelsea," Nicky said slowly, "you see what he's doing, right?"

Chelsea nodded. "I thought I did. But the next day, he never called. I waited, then I called him. No answer. Hours passed. By the time evening rolled around, I knew it wasn't happening. And when he finally called at 8:00 p.m., acting like everything was normal, I wanted to scream."

"What did he say?"

"That he had a flat on his bike and had to walk eight miles in the heat with barely any water."

Nicky looked disgusted. "Wow. He's either a liar or a martyr."

Chelsea shrugged. "I asked if I misunderstood our plans. He apologized and said he thought we weren't definite. But something about the way he said it felt off—too cheerful, too dismissive."

"That's because he didn't care enough to prioritize you. Girl, I've said it before and I'll say it again—if a man doesn't make you a priority early on, he never will."

"I wanted to give him the benefit of the doubt. So I tried to let it go. But the next day, I didn't call. I was still upset. And guess what—he called me, full of attitude."

Nicky's eyebrows shot up. "Wait, so now he's mad?"

"Oh yeah. He said I should've called him back, that if we're going to work, we need to talk things through. He went on this whole rant about how he doesn't want drama, just peace."

"Peace for him or peace for you?"

Chelsea laughed, but it was hollow. "That's the thing. He talks a good game. But his actions never quite match."

The food arrived, but neither of them touched it.

"I even wrote him an email later that week," Chelsea admitted. "I was honest. Told him I was frustrated, confused, and felt like I was chasing something that wasn't chasing me back."

"And?"

"He replied with a cold, formal message about how I needed to be patient. Said he's private and that this takes time."

Nicky shook her head. "And then?"

Chelsea looked down. "Then the texts became fewer. Shorter. Colder. Until eventually, there was nothing."

Silence.

That was the part Chelsea couldn't shake. Not the lies. Not the distance. But the silence. The way he just . . . vanished. Like she meant nothing at all.

"You didn't deserve that," Nicky said, her voice soft now. "None of it."

"I thought I was being too emotional. Too demanding."

"No. You were being real. Open. Honest. And he wasn't man enough to handle it."

Chelsea let out a long breath. "I just don't get how someone can go from saying they're 'compelled to be with you' to acting like you never existed."

Nicky picked up her fork. "Because people say what they think you want to hear sometimes. But the truth always lies in what they do."

They ate in silence for a while.

"Do you think God is using this?" Chelsea asked. "Like . . . maybe his silence is the answer I've been praying for?"

"I do," Nicky said. "But I also think your healing won't come from understanding him. It's going to come from remembering who you are."

Chelsea gave her a half-smile. "I just wish I hadn't fallen so hard."

"Girl, everyone falls. Just don't stay down."

As they wrapped up, Nicky flagged down the waitress for a slice of double chocolate cake—extra whipped cream.

"Trust me," she said. "This'll help more than a text ever could."

Chelsea laughed. It wasn't the carefree kind—but it was genuine. And maybe, for tonight, that was enough.

Chapter Fifteen

Letters I'll Never Send

Langston kicked off his sneakers at the door and made a beeline to the shower. He was frustrated. Even a three-mile run couldn't quiet his thoughts about Chelsea. Each step only made the silence louder.

God, why can't I get this woman out of my mind?

Steam filled the bathroom as the water cascaded over his face. Still, Chelsea's face lingered. Her laugh. Her eyes. The last time he held her.

* * *

Miles away, Chelsea knelt at the side of her bed.

"Father," she whispered, "thank You for this day. I know Your Word says the steps of the righteous are ordered by You, so . . . You must be in this somehow. But I'm struggling. I don't understand why this is happening. Is there something You're trying to teach me—or him? Whatever it is, help me see it. Help me release it. Please, God . . . I need peace tonight. I haven't had a good night's sleep in days. I love You. Amen."

She climbed into bed, determined to rest. But as soon as her head hit the pillow, the images came. His voice. Nicky's voice. Her own thoughts spiraling into doubt.

Why, Langston? Why would you shut me out like this? All I ever wanted . . . was to love you.

She turned over. Again. And again. Every time she tried to quiet her mind, it pushed harder.

God, didn't I beg You for sleep tonight?

Finally, she threw the covers back and turned on the light. Her iPhone sat on the nightstand, tempting her.

No. Don't do it. Don't reread that email. Don't rehash it all.

She looked around, desperate for something to comfort her.

Her eyes landed on the journal resting quietly on the bench by the window. She reached for it, took a deep breath, and opened to a blank page.

If he wouldn't listen, maybe God would. Perhaps the act of writing would be enough.

Dear Langston,

I'm writing because I don't understand. One minute you were here—daily, present, intentional. The next, gone. No warning. No explanation. Just silence.

I thought we were building something real. You told me to share my heart, so I did. But the moment I opened it, you vanished.

I didn't write to start an argument. I wrote because I was hurting. Because texting isn't enough for me. Because I was trying to meet you halfway. You once said our communication was unacceptable and needed to change. I believed you. I adjusted for you. I compromised. But it still wasn't enough.

And now you're gone.

How does someone disappear like that and still claim to care? You spoke of kindness and respect as if they were non-negotiable. But that's not how I feel now. I feel abandoned.

I'm not angry. I'm hurt. I feel foolish for letting my guard down. For believing you were different. I trusted you because you were introduced to me by someone I respected. I felt safe enough to be vulnerable with you—a rare thing for me. But your silence has left me questioning everything.

I'm not asking for much—just an answer. What happened? Why did you treat me this way?

I've prayed for you. Worried about you. Wrestled for peace. And tonight, I'm choosing to let this out—not for a response, but because holding it in is breaking me.

I hope you find balance. I hope you find rest. I hope the next woman doesn't have to walk this road.

~Chelsea

When she finished writing, Chelsea closed her journal, whispering a final prayer.

"God, let this stay between You and me. Heal the parts of me that still ache. And if I was just one chapter in his story, please don't let it repeat with someone else."

Tears slipped quietly down her cheeks as she turned off the light. And for the first time in three days, she fell asleep—not in his arms, but in God's.

* * *

Langston sat on the edge of his bed, Bible open in his lap. His eyes rested on Isaiah 40:31: "But those who trust in the Lord will find new strength. They will soar high on wings like eagles. They will run and not grow weary. They will walk and not faint."

He read the words again, his heart heavy.

God, I'm so tired. Tired of pretending. Tired of carrying it all. I've spent my whole life trying to be perfect—pushing, performing, proving. And now, I can't even figure out how to love properly.

He closed his eyes.

I asked You for a woman like her—and now that she's here, I don't know how to handle it. What if I mess this up? What if she sees the real me and walks away?

His thoughts raced. He walked to his laptop and opened a blank message. For a long moment, he just stared at the screen.

Should I say it? Can I even explain this?

He began to type.

Chelsea,

I don't know how to say this because I've never done anything like it before. I've been distant. I know. And I'm sorry.

Since I met you, I've had to confront things I buried a long time ago—who I am, who I pretend to be, and the parts I'm still afraid to show. I've lived most of my life behind walls. You make me want to come out from behind them.

As a preacher's kid, I was raised in a glass house. Every move was watched. Every mistake amplified. And I stuttered. Badly. So I worked relentlessly to overcome it—perfect diction, perfect performance, perfect posture. I became the man everyone expected. But somewhere along the way, I stopped allowing people to see the parts of me that weren't polished.

Until you.

You shook something in me. The last time I held you, something in me softened and unraveled. I didn't know a woman could feel like home.

Chelsea, I've been quiet because I'm scared. Scared of what you might see if you ever truly saw me. Not the public speaker. Not the polished man. Just me.

But I miss you. I miss your voice. Your spirit. Your

honesty. I miss how you made me feel—safe, seen, real.

I don't know where this letter will land. But I need you to know: I love you. I've never said that to anyone before. I've never felt this before. It's terrifying, exhilarating, and strange in all the best ways.

You've reached a part of me I didn't know existed. And if you can still see something in me worth trying for, I'd like to try.

~Langston

He read it twice. Then again. He hovered his finger over the "Send" button.

God, is this the right thing? Am I too late?

He hesitated, his heart pounding.

Then, slowly, he moved the mouse to the left—and hit "Delete."

Langston shut the laptop, turned off the lights, and lay in the dark. No words—just silence.

A silence heavier than ever.

Chapter Sixteen

Fill Your Horn with Oil

At 7:27 a.m., Chelsea rolled over. "Oh, God, thank You," she said. "Finally, a whole night of sleep." It wasn't easy. She kept waking up in the middle of the night but refused to open her eyes. Chelsea knew that if she opened her eyes for a minute to check the time, she would start thinking about her situation with Langston, and that would be the end of a good night's sleep.

When she rolled over, she heard her phone beep.

A text. Could it be? Is it Langston? Did he decide to stop torturing me with his silence?

With the excitement of a three-year-old discovering candy for the first time, Chelsea reached over and grabbed her cell phone.

Ahhh . . . man, it's not you.

To her dismay, it wasn't Langston. It was Maya, who had recently begun checking in with her a few times a day to see how she was holding up. Both Loretta and Maya had become her crutches, reminding her that there was a purpose in this, as they believed Langston would eventually do right by her.

They had to believe because Chelsea no longer did. All she wanted was to know why. They seemed to think that he was afraid of a relationship and was trying to decide if he wanted to commit to a deep one. Loretta thought that he must have been hurt before and still had some baggage.

But the truth of the matter was that none of their speculations or theories was helping her now. What she really wanted to know was why, after only seven measly weeks, she had gotten so deep. What happened to guarding her heart? What happened to being cautious?

God, why? I know I keep asking You that, but I just really need to know.

Chelsea sighed.

I already know, don't I? It's been so long since I've actually been interested in someone. I was starved for love and just threw caution to the wind at the first sign of something really promising, didn't I? And the floodgates were opened. Now, I'm paying the price.

Chelsea clenched her teeth.

I was so much better off when I didn't allow any room for that. Working sixteen-hour days—being tired from shuttling the boys around, counseling other women, listening to everyone else's woes— that all sounds like paradise compared to how I feel right now. At least running like a maniac allowed me to avoid focusing on what I was missing. It was so much easier.

Chelsea wondered what was behind her hectic schedule. Was it about doing God's work, or was it about avoiding dealing with herself?

But I feel so alive when I pour into others. God, I feel like I'm helping renew them and give them new life through hope in You. I know this is my calling and, to be honest, my greatest passion. And if the truth be told . . . when I'm ministering, I feel total peace— like this is what I was created for. But why does this call have to be such a lonely one, God? Why? It's like I'm stuck between a rock and a hard place. It comes with so much heartache, but the pain is greater when I don't do what You called me to do.

God, all I want to do is give back to You. But sometimes it feels like that comes with a price. I'm all alone. Sometimes I'm just so tired of putting everyone's needs before my own, Father. I'm so tired of being at the bottom of my own priority list. When will I have someone by my side to say, "Baby, today it's about you"? When will I have someone here to encourage me when I'm discouraged instead of always being the one doing all the encouraging? When will someone's prayers cover me? When will I have someone just hold me tight and say, "Baby, it's going to be okay, and I love you"? Do I have a right to ask for that, God?

Ministry can be such a lonely place, and everywhere I go, someone needs something. Being a single mom is such a lonely place, and every time I come home, someone needs something. Being a boss is such a lonely place, and every time the phone rings, someone needs something. All my places are lonely, and I'm so tired. Do You care that I need something? I'm sorry, God. I don't mean to take this out You. I'm just tired. I can't help but wonder . . . if people knew the price that we paid, would they look at us differently? Would they? But I guess it's nothing compared to the price You paid for us. I have no right to complain. I should be happy because I have You, Lord, so I'm not alone. But I sure would love to see the physical manifestations of my hopes and dreams. Who is there for me to spend the rest of my life with and give me hope? How long will I have to live like this? How long, Father?

That was really at the heart of this whole situation. It wasn't really about Langston. It was about Chelsea being tired of supporting the world. But this Langston situation was making it so much worse. She had found a degree of peace in being alone, but now that she had a taste of companionship again, her loneliness felt that much more palpable and real. It hurt that much more.

She dared to believe and dared to hope. Everything had seemed so perfect, like a match made in heaven. He was everything that she had prayed for—a man to minister with. He wasn't running away like Tristen. He was a gentleman. He was economically established, intelligent, and well thought of. But he wasn't kind. He wasn't true. He was cold. Well, at least based on his recent actions. So maybe it was time for her to be thankful instead of lamenting. Could she have really built a life with a man like this?

Matthew walked into his mother's room, half asleep. "Mommy, I had a bad dream," he said.

"You did? Why don't we go into your room and talk about it? I'll lie down with you for a while, and you can tell me all about it."

She walked into his room with him and settled into his bed. She held him tight, and he rested in her arms. "Baby, can I ask you a question? Mommy is a little sad right now. What do you do when you're sad?"

His big brown eyes widened as he looked at his mother with a tender, curious expression. "I just call you, Mommy."

Chelsea gently asked, "Really . . . and how does that help?"

"Mommy, you always talk to me and make me feel better." Matthew snuggled a little closer into his mother's arms as if he were home and safe once again.

Chelsea smiled but wondered, Who do I call? I am so used to being the person on the other end. Who do I call? I have God, Loretta, Maya, Jessica, Nicky. I do have people like my prayer partner, Phil, and other friends. Even Tristen, I guess. He's been trying to resurface as a friend. I should be happy.

But for some reason, at that moment, she did not feel much better.

She began to rub Matthew's head softly and sing one of his favorite Bible songs to him. Before she could ask him about his dream, he dozed off into a deep sleep. She just lay with him and held on tightly. She was so grateful to have her children. They always seemed to help her through just by being there. Yes, they often stressed her out, but they gave her a reason to live.

Just as she began to doze off with Matthew, she heard her cell phone ring.

Who could this be so early in the morning? she thought.

Chelsea tucked Matthew in and headed back to her room to grab the phone. It was a number she didn't recognize.

Oh, brother, what now? she thought.

She picked it up just in case it was someone who needed her. It was always about that "just in case."

"Hello," Chelsea said.

"Reverend Chelsea? This is Samantha Lewis from the church. Do you remember me? I came to one of your divorce ministry meetings. I wanted to call you with a praise report."

Chelsea racked her brain for a moment, trying to remember who this was. She had quite a few women from the church who called her. She could never turn away someone in need, especially since she had been in the same situation during her divorce. Her assistant pastor, who didn't know her well, had embraced her with open arms. Not only did she agree to counsel her, but she even gave Chelsea her home number in case of emergency. Although Chelsea wouldn't dream of calling her, she was touched that she would make herself so available to a relative stranger. As a result of Reverend Jacqueline's love and ministry, Chelsea vowed that when she became ordained, she too would always be there for anyone in need of help. Little did she know what a significant commitment that would turn out to be.

As Samantha began to talk, Chelsea started to place her.

Wait a minute—she's the lady who's going through a really

rough divorce that I spoke to over the phone several times over the last few months. Oh boy, she's also the lady who cried throughout the entire divorce ministry meeting last month.

Chelsea remembered speaking to Samantha for hours, praying with her and encouraging her. When Samantha finally made it to one of the ministry meetings, she spent most of the evening crying. Her pain was so deep it was palpable. Chelsea prayed for her strength and held her tight that evening. The other women also supported her as she tried to find her way through the pain.

Samantha continued, "I have such a praise report that I have to tell you about, Reverend Chelsea. I saw you in church last week, and you rushed out."

Oh, yeah, she thought. That service created a little trouble between her and Langston. That was the one he texted her about when he saw her online.

She refocused on Sister Samantha.

"Reverend Chelsea, I just wanted to thank you for all that you have instilled in me. You are such an inspiration. You kept telling me to hold on and that God was marinating me so that I could emerge as something new amidst everything. You said to stand still and hold on by faith. I know that I don't really know you, but I could feel your spirit and trusted it. I hold onto the words of people I trust. I know that there are many people of the cloth who are very different from what they present, but I can see that you have a good spirit and truly mean well for me and others."

Thank You, Father, Chelsea thought. Even in the midst of my pity party, You give me hope and something to hold onto.

"Rev, you encouraged me, and your words came true. God

was working throughout it all. My soon-to-be ex-husband called me a couple of days ago and said that he had just come home from vacation—I know he mentioned that to be hurtful, to let me know he was with his girlfriend. I don't understand why he has to be so cruel. He told me that he is no longer going to pay our mortgage as of the first of the month. That's in two weeks, Reverend Chelsea. I didn't know what I was going to do. I am trying to take care of my mother, who is in a nursing home, and I can't afford the house and all the utilities. I didn't know what I was going to do.

I remembered what you said and decided to trust God by faith, knowing that He is working, even if I can't see it. He is working! Well, I let go, as you advised, and stood still, and the very next day, my house sold. It had been on the market for five months, Reverend Chelsea, and it sold instantly after I let go. The woman buying it is recently divorced. She needed a house, and I know my house will be a blessing to her. Even in this, I am blessing someone. I don't care if ten other people make me an offer—I am going to sell it to her so that I can bless her.

On top of that, I ran into someone else in the divorce ministry at church a couple of weeks ago. She said she is hurting and wants to die. She has even had thoughts of suicide. I listened. I encouraged her. Can you imagine? Do you remember how weak I was? I couldn't even make it through the meeting without crying, and now, look at God—I am the one helping other women.

And Reverend, after that I saw another sister from the ministry. She was in a dark place—suicidal. And I helped her too. Me—the same woman who couldn't see through her own tears. I became her light.

My Lord, I thank you for the prayers, the encouragement, and the inspiration you gave me, and how you helped me go on when I didn't think I could. I didn't even get mad at my soon-to-be ex-husband. I just prayed that God would convict his heart. Thank you, Reverend Chelsea."

Tears began to well up in Chelsea's eyes as Sister Samantha spoke. Here she was, hurting, and the same words that God laid on her heart to give this woman months ago were what she herself needed today. Why couldn't she stand still? She kept hearing God say, "Stand still," but she felt like she had to move. Maybe that was the problem. If she had stood still from the beginning, maybe she wouldn't be hurting now. But as she once told Sister Samantha, God is working.

I, too, should just let go and pray that God will work it out as He sees fit. If I never hear from Langston again, then so be it. If he never explains why he walked away and trampled on my feelings, then so be it.

Tears rolled down her face as she thanked God for using Sister Samantha to minister to her. Chelsea said, "Sister Samantha, I am so happy to hear this. Your ministry is now growing. Where you once were weak, God has strengthened you and used you in a mighty way to do his work. I know that there was a time when you didn't even think you could make it or have a reason to live. Sometimes, in what we are going through, death can seem preferable to life. But I am so grateful to God that you held on because now you have become the strength to help others survive. God honored your praise in the midst of your pain and truly delivered you.

"I also want you to know that sometimes you will still have rough days, but never, never, never, never give up. This is just the beginning. Believe me, there is purpose in our pain, and God will not waste even one of our tears. I am so proud of you. You don't know how much you have ministered to and encouraged me today. I was empty, and you filled me. I thank you for that."

Sister Samantha began to weep with a bittersweet joy.

Chelsea said, "Let's pray before we hang up. But this time, you pray."

And she did. Sister Samantha thanked God for all of His help and for allowing her to trust Him by faith. She thanked Him for helping her withstand the thoughts of death and suicide, the brokenness, the hurt, and the pain. Then she thanked God for His angel in Reverend Chelsea. She thanked Him for her words, her ministry, and her strength.

Tears continued to stream down Chelsea's face as Sister Samantha prayed. "Thank you, Sister Samantha. May God bless and keep you."

With that, the two women said goodbye to each other. Chelsea rocked herself back and forth on her bed.

There is a purpose, she thought, *even in the situation with Langston. This will become part of my ministry.*

She heard a voice inside say, *1 Samuel 16.* She opened her Bible and read what it said:

The LORD said to Samuel, "How long will you mourn for Saul, since I have rejected him as king over Israel? Fill your horn with oil and be on your way; I am sending you to Jesse of Bethlehem. I have chosen one of his sons to be king."

"My Lord," she said. "This is not what You want for me. How can I go where You want me to go if I am still mourning what You rejected? If You truly wanted this to be so, then it would be. Look at me—what have I been reduced to over some disappointment? What Langston did to me will be returned to him as You deal with him, but as for me, You know my heart, my intentions, and my deeds. I will be fruitful in the place of my afflictions. It is time to birth something new. How can I give a person so much power over me? Have I not endured far worse? Have I not seen other dreams die, which now I realize would have been nightmares if they had lived?"

Chelsea immediately got off her bed and began to pray. She prayed for strength for the journey ahead. She prayed to forgive and let go; she prayed to trust God in the midst of everything. She even prayed for Langston because she truly didn't know what he was going through right now.

And then she began to write. She wrote in her journal and wrote for the people.

She said, "This will one day help others. I will open my heart and allow my hurt and pain to minister to all those who are hurting and going through it and don't know how they will make it. I will write for all the broken women and men who are stuck."

She still didn't know how her story would end.

She didn't know if Langston would ever come back—or if she even wanted him to.

She didn't know if the house she had claimed eight years ago would ultimately be the place she'd raise her children.

She didn't know if God would grant her the daughter her heart longed for.

She didn't know if her career would ever feel truly fulfilling.

She didn't know if she'd one day stand before the nations

and preach the gospel.

She didn't know if "happily ever after" was still possible.

But what she did know was that her life wasn't so bad.

She had gone from almost nothing to more than she'd ever imagined.

From searching for a place to lay her head while five months pregnant and alone to living in a four-bedroom home she had once only dreamed of.

From juggling two jobs to survive to one role that paid more than both combined.

From heartbreak and trauma to helping broken people find healing through Christ.

From wanting to die to wanting to live again.

From barely making it to becoming an ordained minister, with two master's degrees, two beautiful sons, a circle of true friends, and—above all—hope.

Chelsea wiped the tears from her eyes, rose from the floor, and stepped into the hallway.

She began running through the house, praising God out loud.

Not because everything made sense.

But because He had carried her through it all.

Chapter Seventeen

Seven Weeks to Surrender

Chelsea still had her ups and downs after the whole Langston thing. She knew she shouldn't let it break her, but it had now been a full two and a half weeks since she had heard from him. Today was a down day. She sat on a plane bound for Vancouver on business, and after four hours in the air, the stillness had become torture.

There was something about being motionless that disturbed her. When she moved, she didn't have to face reality—her heartbreak, her guilt, or God. When she moved, she could lose herself in her children, her work, her ministry, and her friends. But when she sat still, she had to confront herself. And that hurt.

Where do I even go from here? she wondered.

Stuck in her seat, she wrestled with the "could've, would've, should've" scenarios of the last few weeks.

What if I hadn't sent that email? What if I'd been content with how things were? Would I still be frustrated by what was lacking? Or would I be here, thankful for even the smallest of texts? Was I too demanding?

She thought of one of Langston's last messages: Thanks for opening up and being so transparent with me. I, too, feel very moved by who and what you are. Understand, I'm a very private person, and this will take some time for me . . . and us. So we must pace ourselves and be patient.

Maybe if I'd explained how raw I still was from my last long-distance relationship, he might have understood how hard this was for me. Maybe he would've stayed.

The maybes wouldn't stop, but none could change the fact: it was over. She wasn't ready for it to be over. She wasn't ready to let go of a dream she had only just begun to believe in again. And if he wasn't the one, he was a really good counterfeit.

Two more hours passed. The plane—and her thoughts—circled endlessly. The worst part? Knowing that Langston had probably moved on without a backward glance. She thought, *You told me when your dad died, you didn't even miss a beat. So why would I expect you to miss me?*

He had two sides—one tender and sweet, the other cold and calculated. She remembered the biting tone in the columns he wrote for a local paper. "It's just entertainment," he'd said. But was she just entertainment, too?

Can someone really have two such opposite halves? Sooner or later, the masks have to fall. Was that what happened? When the pilot finally announced the descent into Vancouver, it was music to her ears. She couldn't wait to be distracted—by the city, by people, by anything other than herself.

Customs brought another long wait. Another stretch of silence. Another war in her head. *God, I'm going to trust You and let go.* Why hold on to someone who chose to leave? She thought back to every breakup she'd ever initiated. Had she ever hurt someone this coldly?

Bradley, maybe — the doctor with two sides: calm competence in the hospital, chaos in the quiet corners of their relationship. He had seemed unstable. This . . . this was different. This felt like betrayal. Just as her mind spun into another spiral, her phone rang. Thomas. A musician from church who had once offered to coach her in vocals.

"Hey, T," she said, grateful for the interruption.

He'd called with a business idea about opening a boarding school for inner-city youth. After a quick brainstorm, he shifted the conversation.

"Chelsea, I'm believing God to bring someone very special

into your life."

"How ironic," she muttered. "I thought He already did." She opened up and told him the story, swearing him to secrecy.

"Chelsea," Thomas said, "you have a beautiful spirit. If I could see it the first time I met you, so could he. Maybe he's just processing. Or maybe . . . he was a precursor to your blessing." He paused, then added, "Before the real blessing, a counterfeit or a preview often shows up. Like John the Baptist before Jesus. Either way, trust God. This man will either return changed—or he simply wasn't meant for you."

That word stayed with her. She remembered the dream she'd had the night before her final email to Langston. In it, she was in a hospital, staring at a 3D sonogram screen. Two babies hugging in her womb.

Twins. She'd woken thinking, I have to tell Langston. How could I dream that . . . and he still leave?

She pushed the thought down. Her cab pulled up to the hotel. Her room wasn't ready, so she went to the café and found a window seat overlooking the mountains and sea. The view was breathtaking—and achingly romantic.

The pianist began to play "It Is Well." Then "Amazing Grace." Chelsea smiled.

God, You haven't given up on me. Thank You.

The comfort didn't last long. Jessica, her college roommate, called. They caught up, then dove straight into heartbreak confessions. Jessica, too, had experienced the vanishing act—men who fled without explanation. Chelsea listened, grateful for the solidarity.

"They always come back," Jessica declared.

"Do you think Langston will?" Chelsea asked quietly.

Jessica laughed. "Let him try. As soon as you finish the last spoonful of your Häagen-Dazs, it's over."

Chelsea laughed too, but her thoughts circled back. Would she even want Langston back? Could she trust him again? She didn't think so.

Later, Chelsea called Loretta, who reminded her not to waste her trip sulking in a hotel room.

"Someone in Vancouver might need to hear about Jesus, and you're hiding out because of a man who's not even thinking about you."

The words stung.

Was she failing God by mourning?

She lay in bed, replaying Langston's voice in her head. He'd once said he prayed for her daily. Was that a lie, too?

God, am I being punished for not letting go? she wondered. Like Moses missing the Promised Land?

Overcome, Chelsea threw a pillow and screamed, "JUST STOP IT! You're supposed to be stronger than this. You've helped so many people. Why can't you help yourself?"

A wave of shame and grief crushed her. Thoughts swirled—too fast, too cruel. Wouldn't it be better if you were dead? No, she told herself. Just shut up.

She clutched her phone, debating whether to call anyone. Finally, she dialed Maya.

Without hesitation, Maya answered.

"I need help," Chelsea said. "I feel like a failure. I want to reach out to him, but I know I shouldn't."

"Chelsea, you're grieving," Maya said gently. "Stop expecting yourself to be superhuman. This man was poison to your system, and like you said, he awakened something that had been buried. You were starving for love. You took in too much too fast, and now you're sick."

Chelsea cried quietly.

"Your mistake wasn't loving—it was giving too much, too soon. But you're no longer starving. The next time love comes, you'll be ready."

Then Maya gasped. "Chelsea, you said it lasted seven weeks."

"Yeah, why?"

"Seven is God's number of completion. God shut the door after seven weeks. Don't you see? He spared you."

Chelsea blinked. The weight of that truth settled in.

God had shut the door—for her protection. She began to understand: this man was a mirage, a preparation. Nothing more.

They prayed together and said goodnight. Chelsea fell asleep lighter than she had in days. A week later, on the flight home, Chelsea felt different. Stronger. Clearer. Every time her mind drifted back to Langston, she whispered, "Seven. Completion."

She didn't know why it ended the way it did, but she knew it would be okay.

There was a sermon in all of this, or maybe a new chapter of her life waiting to unfold. Either way, the best was still to come. And back home, life hadn't paused. Her son had been called names on the football field. Her ex dropped the ball on sponsorship forms. Her parents were struggling, her sister and nephew had barely survived a car accident, and two friends were dealing with job loss and pregnancy drama. And Chelsea had a sermon to prepare.

Real life was calling. No more pity party.

She smiled.

Thanks, God, for this time to regroup. I leave it all in Your hands, and I won't take it back.

As she reclined in her upgraded first-class seat, Chelsea whispered, "God, You are awesome."

Already Won

Chelsea sat on the bleachers between Nia and Rosa, bundled in a blanket against the crisp fall air. It was the last football game of the season—a finale that marked more than the end of touchdowns and tailgates. It symbolized the close of a tumultuous year: one marked by heartbreak, healing, rediscovery, and quiet resilience. Maybe, just maybe, it marked the beginning of something new.

She smiled as she watched Daniel sprint across the field, her voice joining the chorus of cheers in the stadium. He looked up, caught her eye, and grinned.

"That's my baby," she said aloud, pride swelling in her chest. This year had been hard-earned and hard-won. Between serving at church, raising two boys solo, and juggling ministry and motherhood, Chelsea had lived each day like it was a championship. She had hidden jeans and a jersey under her clergy robe just to make kickoff. She had laughed, cried, collapsed—and stood again.

But most of all, she had grown.

Laughter flowed freely between her and her closest football mom friends—Nia and Rosa, now more like sisters. From late-night texts to shared school pickups, they had become a tribe built on faith, friendship, and fierce loyalty.

"So you're taking Hebrew now?" Rosa asked, nearly choking on her nachos.

Chelsea nodded. "Why not? I want to preach with depth. Know the original text. Maybe even understand myself a little more in the process."

Rosa laughed. "You and those big dreams."

Chelsea didn't laugh this time. She looked out across the golden horizon, where the clouds curled like ancient scrolls.

"It's more than a dream," she said softly. "One day, I'll be in the fields. Africa. India. Somewhere. Holding babies who've never felt God's love. Preaching in places where hope is scarce. That's what I want."

"Do the men in prison ever hit on you?" Nia teased, trying to lighten the moment.

Chelsea chuckled. "No, not really. It's actually humbling. They remind me of what restoration looks like when we stop running from God. I just want to give hope. Even if it's just to one soul."

Suddenly, Nia's husband shouted, "Chelsea! Daniel just sacked the quarterback!"

Chelsea jumped up. "Go, Daniel! That's my baby!"

Ricky, Rosa's husband, laughed. "That happened ten minutes ago."

"Late or not, he's still my boo!"

They all laughed together. These were the moments Chelsea lived for—the ordinary holy ones. The ones where she wasn't reverend or counselor or strong single mother. Just Chelsea, fully seen and surrounded.

Matthew plopped onto her lap, sweaty and beaming. "Mommy! I scored two touchdowns in my game!"

"What's your name again?"

"Matthew Touchdown Rocket Baller Stevens!"

Chelsea laughed and kissed his forehead. "You sure did, baby. Here's five dollars. Snack bar run—but only after a big, fat kiss."

"Mom! There's no kissing in football!" But he kissed her cheek anyway and ran off.

Then Rosa leaned in. "So…have you heard from Langston?"

Chelsea hesitated. "No. It's been almost three months. But I stopped waiting a long time ago. Oddly enough, someone else reached out."

At that, Nia turned fully toward her. "Who? Spill."

Chelsea pulled out her phone and opened an email. "Brace yourselves. I got this two days ago. From Tristen."

Chelsea took a breath, still feeling its weight in her chest.

Chelsea,

This morning I woke up with you in my heart. I dreamed we were married on a secluded beach. Just you and me. You cried as we talked about all we'd been through and how God brought us back together. I held you, and it felt like home.

Now that my cancer's in remission, maybe we can finally get this right. I still love you.

~Tristen

The silence that followed wasn't awkward—it was reverent.

Chelsea looked down. "The beach. That's my safe place. How did he know?"

"So what now?" Rosa asked.

"I don't know. Maybe it's timing. Maybe it's God. Or maybe . . . it's just clarity."

Chelsea had learned some things. She had fallen for a man's representative, not his reality. She had learned that timing without purpose is poison, and that sometimes, God's greatest gifts are the ones that never arrive.

"I've watched people fall in love. I've walked them through breakups. And I always say—love reveals itself in time. In the beginning, people send their best actor, not their truest self."

She exhaled.

"There's nothing worse than forcing something out of season. It's like biting into unripe fruit. I'll wait for my due season."

Nia nodded. "Your season is coming."

Chelsea smiled. "And when it does, I want someone who doesn't flinch at my strength or silence my spirit. Someone who can lead—or follow—with humility."

As the game ended and families scattered, Collin picked up the boys. Jessica left for pizza with David. Rosa and Nia headed to baseball practice.

Chelsea drove home humming praise music. She exhaled into the quiet.

Then she saw him.

Langston.

On her doorstep.

Her breath caught.

He stood slowly, slipping his phone into his pocket. "Chelsea, I know this is unexpected, but we need to talk."

Chelsea didn't speak. Her eyes scanned his face. Was it regret? Hope? Fear?

She looked up at the sky. God, is this You? Or is this a test?

Whatever the answer, she was no longer afraid. She had cried, healed, prayed, and risen. She didn't need closure to walk in peace. She didn't need a man to complete her joy. She had already won.

And now, she was finally ready . . . for whatever came next.

The Knock

Chelsea's journal lay open, but she hadn't written a word. The air was still, her spirit calm, but her mind was anything but.

Langston's unexpected visit replayed in her head like a looping film. His eyes had said more than his words ever could.

Yet even as she stood there hours later, sorting through the swirl of what-ifs, her phone buzzed.

Unknown Caller

She answered without thinking. "Hello?"

A pause.

Then a voice she hadn't heard in months. "Chelsea, it's me. Tristen."

She stood up straighter, the air suddenly charged. "Hey, I wasn't expecting—"

"I know," he said, his voice soft. "But I needed to hear your voice."

She closed her eyes. The timing. The tension. The tenderness of it all.

Was this divine orchestration—or a test of her resolve?

As Tristen spoke, the words from her unfinished journal entry came back to her:

I will dance again. Not because I was never broken, but because I am no longer bound.

She wasn't sure what the future held.

Langston stood at the threshold. Tristen echoed hope from afar.

But Chelsea? Chelsea was here. Whole. Healed. Standing on bones that once made her fall.

This wasn't the end.

It was the beginning . . . of her dance.

Acknowledgments

First and foremost, I must acknowledge Jesus, my Lord and Savior—the One who strengthened me, sustained me, and placed within me a faith that knows how to stand, a heart that knows how to love, and the courage to keep moving forward with hope and joy.

To my parents, whose unwavering love, prayers, and example helped shape the woman I am today—thank you for grounding me in faith, love, and the values that have carried me forward.

To my sons, Jayson and Christian—you are my greatest gifts. I have always sought to live as a woman of faith, a mother led by love, and a business leader marked by integrity and resilience. May my life—and these pages—reflect what it means to steward God's gifts well, to walk boldly, and to stand firm even when the path is not easy. I pray this book makes you proud and encourages you to live as the men God created you to be.

To my siblings, my family, my friends, and my faith community—thank you for standing with me and for me throughout life. For every prayer prayed, every tear witnessed, every laugh shared, and every joy celebrated together—I am deeply grateful. Life was never meant to be lived alone, and I am richer because of the love, compassion, friendship, and hope you have poured into my life.

And finally, to my publisher, Rev. Taneki—thank you for helping make a dream that lived in my heart for over twenty years a reality. Your love, prayers, and steadfast support were invaluable, and I am deeply grateful for your belief in this work.

And to my readers—thank you for supporting a dream God placed in my heart. By choosing to read these pages, you have become part of the story.

This book is for you.

About *the* Author

Carla Calizaire is a global commercial leader, ordained minister, and storyteller whose life and work are deeply rooted in purpose, people, and the pursuit of lasting impact. Carla has spent her career guiding organizations through growth and renewal—from Fortune 500 healthcare companies to emerging ventures—always leading with integrity, vision, and heart.

As an ordained minister, Carla leads with faith, empathy, and wisdom—inspiring others to see that true leadership goes beyond results; it's about purpose, stewardship, and lasting impact. Her work is anchored in a belief that excellence and compassion can coexist, and that every challenge is an invitation to grow in character and clarity.

A devoted mother to her two sons, Jayson and Christian, Carla's greatest joy is watching them grow into strong and principled men of purpose. Her journey as a mother fuels her passion for mentoring and developing leaders—helping people from all walks of life lead, heal, and rise with grace through life's defining moments.

When she's not building businesses or uplifting others, you'll find Carla exploring new places, sharing stories over good food, and finding beauty in the everyday narratives that connect us all. She makes her home in New Jersey with her sons, and she believes in the storytelling of life—that every path, every trial, and every triumph is part of a masterpiece still being written.

The Beginning of Her Becoming is the first novel in *The Becoming of Her* series—a three-book journey through heartbreak, healing, and the holy work of becoming. Chelsea's story continues in *The Breaking of Her Becoming* and concludes in *The Rising of Her Becoming.*

Also in The Becoming of Her Series

A trilogy of *beginning, breaking, and rising*—the sacred, unhurried work of a woman coming home to herself.

Book One: *The Beginning of Her Becoming*

Book Two: *The Breaking of Her Becoming*

Book Three: *The Rising of Her Becoming*

Connect with Carla at carlacalizaire.com
Instagram @carlacalizaire